TARRY THIS NIGHT

KRISTYN DUNNION

ARSENAL PULP PRESS
VANCOUVER

TARRY THIS NIGHT
Copyright © 2017 by Kristyn Dunnion

ARSENAL PULP PRESS
Suite 202 – 211 East Georgia St.
Vancouver, BC V6A 1Z6
Canada
arsenalpulp.com

The publisher gratefully acknowledges the support of the Canada Council for the Arts and the British Columbia Arts Council for its publishing program; and the Government of Canada, and the Government of British Columbia (through the Book Publishing Tax Credit Program), for its publishing activities.

This is a work of fiction. Any resemblance of characters to persons either living or deceased is purely coincidental.

Cover and text design by Oliver McPartlin
Cover photo by Didier Descouens
Edited by Susan Safyan

Printed and bound in Canada

Library and Archives Canada Cataloguing in Publication:
Dunnion, Kristyn, 1969-, author
    Tarry this night / Kristyn Dunnion.

Issued in print and electronic formats.
ISBN 978-1-55152-705-5 (softcover).—ISBN 978-1-55152-706-2
(HTML)
    I. Title.
PS8557.U552T37 2017   C813'.6   C2017-904063-4
                                                C2017-904064-2

Lamentations: for my sighs are many,

and my heart is faint.

Naomi advises the widowed and impoverished Ruth concerning Boaz, a wealthy landowner: "Tarry this night, and it shall be in the morning, that if he will perform unto thee the part of a kinsman, well; let him do the kinsman's part: but if he will not do the part of a kinsman to thee, then will I do the part of a kinsman to thee, as the LORD liveth: lie down until the morning."

—The Book of Ruth, King James Bible

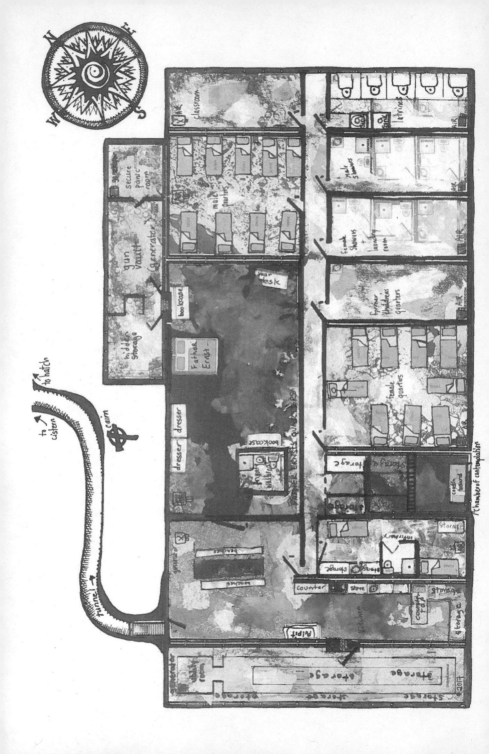

CHAPTER 1

They finish the salt pork first. Then the jarred pickerel, flats of canned beans, strips of cured venison. Dried fruit, flattened like tongues, loosens their molars when they tear into it. In the last drum of corn-grit flour, they discover an infestation of weevils that they sift out and chew carefully, along with their nymphs, the beaded strings and fine-powdered clumps of their nests. By the time Cousin Paul gets orders to don topside gear—sand-coloured coveralls with sleeves, insulated gloves, UV hood—and laces up the Family's last pair of boots, the rest having been unstitched and simmered for broth, all that remains in the food stores is a third of a barrel of mouldy oats. That, for eleven bellies.

Cousin Ruth walks the narrow tunnel with Paul. She shakes Father Ernst's iron key ring, making a kind of tin music. They pause in the dark at the foot of the Mission Pole ladder. A pipe drips.

"Won't last a month," says Paul.

"We shall, God willing," says Ruth.

She cleans the eye windows on his gas mask with the hem of her shirt. Sees his cheek tremor. He loves and hates to go. "Mind the heathens, the landmines." She doesn't mention last time or the previous provider.

"I'll be fine."

Paul takes the key ring and shoulders his rifle. He climbs twenty reinforced metal rungs up the riser hatch ahead of her. He inserts one long key, grabs the pull handle, and slides the deadbolt on the interior blast lid. Ruth is halfway, dizzy from the shift in air pressure. Her palms slip with sweat. On the thirteenth rung, her puny biceps begin to shake. Paul breaks the seal on the riser lip and pushes the heavy door up, open. Keys jangle. Dust and silt rain down, coating Ruth's face and hair. She spits. Paul climbs over, he's out. She can't see him and panic blooms in her chest. His boots thud against the outer hatch, quiet thunder. Ruth's feet feel for rungs, her hand stretches.

"Help," she cries.

Paul reaches and pulls her the last bit. He says, "How'll you get back down?"

"God will carry me. That, or I'll jump."

Ruth kneels in the cramped cave to catch her breath while Paul checks the bunker's ventilation pipes—intake, outflow, septic drain pump—and the blast valves that protect their ears and internal organs from any nearby explosions.

"Check again when I get back," he says. "You okay?"

She nods. "Filters."

"Yep. Warfare gas carbon adbsorbers. Can't scavenge those."

"Mayhap."

Paul peers through wide-angle viewer ports on the cave's external door, scans left to right and back. Ruth pushes and he lets her look. No jackals or wild dogs, no marauding bands of godless sinners. Just the relentless shock of sun and miles of burning sand, a boundless shimmer broken once, faraway, by a sharp white cliff, like bone puncturing skin.

"Stay out of trouble, Ruth. Check on Rebekah?" Paul flattens her to his chest, squeezes air from her rattling lungs with thin arms.

"Call that a hug," she says, but really, every inch of her body sings.

This is it. Paul adjusts his mask and slings the rifle. Ruth ties a rag over her nose and mouth. He inserts the largest key of all and cranks the outer bolt, loosens the cam latch that seals the blast shield to the frame. It sticks. Sticks. Gives.

A rapier of light stabs their underworld. Dust motes spark and swirl. Paul pushes the heavy door, and sun fills the widening gap. Sun heats the space between Ruth's feet. Sun licks Ruth's hands at her hips. One more heave and the door stands wide. Paul is a dazzled burst of soldier in military gear, blanched pure as God's breath. Light blows Ruth's retinas; she squints against the red-orange spirals that slice her eyelids. Paul's shadow blankets her. Wind stirs her hair. This is a demon choir, temptation, an eruption of song on the body. She's sun drunk and reckless, such that a furtive picture fills her—Cousin Paul returning with signs and portents for the Ascension and the Family rising to their due glory. Inside the nutshell of that dream, the meat: she and Paul betrothed, preparing the holy union ceremony.

If Father Ernst doesn't claim her first.

Last thing—Father Ernst's orders—she tosses Paul the box of ammo. He pockets it. Then Paul's slow wave, and his shadow disappears. Nothing but dry heat, the burning spires of an infinite summer. The urge to hurtle herself after him, to let her flesh char to ash in the unforgiving sand, overwhelms. Paul shuts the outer door, and that solemn blow is a belly punch. Ruth slides the bolt. The cam latch sucks to reseal. She tumbles the keys into her pocket. Must return them to Father Ernst, who waits.

She's blind, blinder than before, and desolate. The dark eats her.

Skin cools, breath slows, hands steady. Still, an ember glows inside: sun-dazzle legacy, the scorch. Yea, that wind and fire beget a yearning.

Ruth feels her way back down the tunnel, knife in hand. Anything could breach the bunker in those vulnerable moments. Last time Paul left at night, and a disoriented bat flew down the hatch, which Ruth hunted for days. The singularly outstanding adventure in her years below. There. Ruth intuits movement. Something holds and scampers in small bursts. Nowadays no one's ever sad to see a rat, but years ago Father Ernst went mad trying to locate their entry point. If rodents slipped in, so might disease, poison gas, infidels.

Ruth checks the first and second tunnel traps, ten feet apart: empty. Something snacked the bait, tiny fabric scraps soaked in her own blood. She fashioned the traps by nailing springs from a rusted-out cot to wooden platforms. Paul asked why she didn't set the bar on two of them, how she intended to catch anything if they weren't spring-loaded. She only smiled. Her third trap is tripped and wriggling. *Praise be!* Ruth holds the furred body and releases the hammer and spring bar, which has trapped the rat's face, crushing part of its soft skull. Whiskers twitch in her fingers and Ruth catches the shine from one desperate eye. Incredibly, it is still alive. "I've fed you twice," she says, breaking its neck. "Now it's your turn." She tucks her knife back into the sturdy pouch that rides her belt. She guesses a two-pounder, and drops the carcass in her sack.

Meat in the gruel tonight.

Halfway between the Mission Pole and the Great Hall she kneels at the cairn. A dim light flickers above their communal headstone. She loves this lonely spot and not just because Paul built it. Here lie sacred cousin remains: cinders and dust, a handful of indigestible charred bits, twisted locks of hair. Everything else is purposed. Flesh to dry, organs to fry, and bones to nourish the broth.

She prays. "Holy Father in Heaven, watch over us. Especially Cousin Paul, wheresoever Your light finds him. Bring him back, righteous and safe, as You see fit. Cherish our martyrs, whose spirits tend the great garden, awaiting Your command, Amen."

Ruth fingers the letters scratched into their piece of slate. Strange to see her own name spelled out on the cairn, as though she, too, is buried alongside her namesake, the original Mother. Her favourite, Memaw Ruth—Father Ernst's first wife, eldest of the cousin mothers and still so much younger than him. Two other mothers died below, one from bad birthing and one shrieking from tumours while she pulled out her hair. A dozen tiny infants never made it past the first croupy months. Thomas never returned from foraging; his unblessed bones lie topside among the heathens. Jeremiah, the subsequent provider who lorded over them, was so badly scorched that his parts, although shaved bit by bit in the infirmary, pussed and frothed until he eventually succumbed to his wounds.

Years ago, when Father Ernst bade him remove a section of tunnel wall to bury the remains, Paul asked why the bunker blueprints hadn't specified a cairn. "Was it an oversight?" Paul asked, causing Father Ernst to redden and roar. "Or were we never meant to lose kin below the earth?" Paul was whipped and shamed and sent to the chamber of contemplation. The Doctrine, as Father Ernst calmly discussed later, is simply not clear about how long the Family must wait.

"There will be signs, there will be portents," says Father Ernst. "There will be an alignment of events, a mystical and material coming together. God will speak to me and send forth a vision for our most glorious Ascension. Then, and only then, shall we rise in all our glory!"

CHAPTER 2

The dinner bell, which once adorned the thick brown neck of Father Ernst's favourite Guernsey, now rings out in the Great Hall. Small feet patter, children's voices bubble, someone drags a wooden bench along the floor. They've heard about the meat: such merriment.

Inside his private quarters, Father Ernst remains kneeling. His lips work in silent prayer. His palms raise, beseeching. The wide sleeves of his robe bunch at the elbows. God listens, of course, but why does He no longer speak? Three hundred days without visions, without Holy messages to guide him. This must be part of the journey. A test. The obvious thing is to have faith. But the pull between tending the Family's daily well-being and dedicating his whole self to divinity grows taut. Somewhere, an answer exists. He runs a hand through tangled hair, tugs the length of his beard. For now, the boy will forage. He'll bring back sustenance: roots and bark and greens. Maybe carrion. If he doesn't return, there'll be one less mouth to feed. Then Father Ernst must choose a martyr.

They will not starve.

Father Ernst stamps his feet and swings his arms. He must throw off this heaviness and join the others. He paces the length of the room. Straightens his Bible, the Doctrine, the framed Family photo, all propped on the war desk. Surveys the room. Everything in its place. He breathes deeply. Opens the door and locks it behind him, drops the keys into the robe's deep pocket.

Voices hush as he approaches. Cousin Silas peddles the stationary bike, activating the generator and air pumps. The boy's efforts spare batteries and preserve system filters, but mostly it keeps him occupied, out of Ernst's way.

Father Ernst bangs his gavel at the head of the table. Silence. He squints around at the mostly blond heads, counting his tribe, sprung mainly from his own loins. Rests at Paul's empty seat, draws a line across the table to Ruth. She's getting big. Pretty, at last.

Hannah places her hand on his. "Husband," she says.

This is private talk, he's told her before. But he leans and kisses her cheek. "Cousin Bride, are you well?"

"Very." She smiles for him.

He says, "Let us pray. Oh, Heavenly Father, we, Your earth army, stay the path of righteous living, following Your Holy example by way of the Doctrine. We pray we may one day ascend in victory to glorify Your Holy name. Thank You for this meal, a gift bestowed most mercifully upon us. We humbly await Your command. Amen."

"Amen," they say.

Father Ernst scrapes his chair to sit. "You may join us, Cousin Silas," he says, and the boy hustles to the bench. He's a good size—thin, of course—but plenty of work left in him. Silas settles, glances surreptitiously at Ruth and Hannah, who remain oblivious. The girls' eyes are trained on Father Ernst, as they should be. Ruth sits tall, tight fists on either side of her bowl—she wants recognition for procuring the meat. Ernst smiles. She will learn to seek praise from more fitting pursuits.

"Mother Susan," he says, and she shuffles to his right side, carrying the dinner tray. She serves him first, one ladle of porridge. Mother Rebekah follows stiffly with half a ladle in his water cup. A dullness inhabits her face, her body. What grievance now? The boys are served down one side of the table, then the girls. Hannah lifts her bowl and Mother Susan dollops a second spoonful to help draw her menses, else the poor girl may never conceive.

"Let us eat," says Father Ernst, and the table livens with movement. All but Ruth, still facing him, one eyebrow arched expectantly. She's a spit for Memaw Ruth, his first wife. That very expression, maddening, hooked his curiosity and quickly imbued in him an unprecedented desire, a profound need: how he strived to please her. He might as well be standing on the farmhouse porch thirty-nine years ago, the way he feels right now. He can still smell that peach pie cooling on the sill, still remember his first glimpse of the girl inside, the way she turned toward the screen at his knock, sun from the kitchen window catching her silhouette and stretching a shadow across the linoleum. Then she was at the door with her eyebrow arched—was it in humour? Was she flirting even then? She looked at his traveller's face, the dust on his hat, in his hair, the mud caked on his boots, the small bag set beside him on the step, prison tag hastily removed and crumpled into his pocket, and she seemed to know in that one glance all he had done in his life, all his fouling and failures, and also his triumphs, pulling himself up from the mire. In an instant she seemed to understand the dearth of gentleness he had experienced up to that moment, and how hungry he was for it. No, famished.

"Husband, will you not eat?"

Father Ernst startles at the voice so close to him, the small hand pressing his. One spoon, one bowl, a watery slop of oats. A table lined with young faces. Women huddle by the kitchen, scraping what's left from a pot, pecking like thin, silent hens. Father Ernst fills his spoon, brings it to his mouth. Oats on his tongue. Counts to ninety, begins to chew. He finds a piece of meat in the next spoonful, holds it between molars as long as he can before softly tearing into it. The women are his wives. This girl, his bride. The children, his tribe. Yes, quite so.

"Shall we have Reflections on the Doctrine?" his young bride asks. Cousin Hannah.

"Of course," he says. He must shake off this weakness, nostalgia. He must focus.

Wives collect the dishes with a great clacking and carry them to the kitchen. Quiet murmurs, the drip and slosh of dishwater.

Father Ernst stands. "We shall begin." He looks to the gusting air vent above and summons the Holy incarnation, that which fuels him. "I have prayed all day, children. I have prayed all night. Know this: we are the exalted tribe. Never question it. We shall have dominion over the earth!"

Cousins say, "Praise be, Father in Heaven, amen."

Father Ernst raises his arms, and his wide sleeves gather. He catches his own stink with the movement. His voice fills the shadowy hall and echoes off the bunker walls. "In the beginning there was darkness and there was the light. The Doctrine sayeth that the earth shall wither. Fields shall dry to drought, fires shall ravage the forests, oceans shall rise to overflow, and coastlines vanish in their excess. Mountains shall crumble and quake."

Cousins say, "Then shall Ye know my time is nigh!"

He shouts, "And the great dragon was cast out of Heaven, that old serpent called the Devil, and Satan, which deceiveth the whole world; he was cast out into the darkness and his angels were cast out with him!"

"Cast out in darkness! Yet we guard the light!"

Susan and Rebekah, finished in the kitchen, tuck onto benches. Rebekah stacks block pieces for her latest quilt on the table, chooses one, and begins to pick at it with a silver needle. Her hand flies steady, up and down. That, and the serpentine movements of the silky embroidery floss, mesmerize the children. Breath wheezes from their open mouths. Father Ernst's sermon—upstaged by a bit of sewing. He passes a hand through his hair. He moves as he talks, touches a small shoulder here, a tousled head there, to draw their attention back.

"You have never known the earth, topside, where Satan reigns. Where dim-witted government heretics revel in depravity. You were born inside our sacred nest, or else brought below as babes. But I know better. As do your mothers."

"Heresy and murder, mayhem and destruction, that which lies above. Amen," they say.

Father Ernst paces the length of the table. "We lived in that contaminated world and tilled the soil, harvested and stored the grain. We dug this refuge, poured the concrete, planned our survival. We worked alongside so many Martyrs in the Great Standoff. We bunkered our faith and sealed shut the doors to temptation."

Cousins sing, "Forty hands high, the roof. Forty hands wide!"

Father Ernst is on track now; he is bringing it home. "We guard the Doctrine!"

Silas shouts, "We guard the Light!"

Father Ernst says, "We are God's glory!"

Silas shouts, "We are the Light!"

Thunder: little feet kick, hands drum the table top, and the Family begins to sing:

"Raise thee, praise thee, upward shall we climb,
Though Satan's pow'r has but an hour and ours eternal shine.
Raise thee, praise thee, upward shall we climb.
Our Father's will protects us still and leads us topside time."

Voices fill the Great Hall. Mother Susan's scratchy soprano floats above, and every now and then thin, crackling notes make themselves known in tuneless wonder—Cousin Silas—otherwise it's an excellent rendition of the Ascension Song. Cousins clap. Blood pumps, skin warms, and vibrations of their joy shimmy fine dust in the air from joints in the support beams, from the trusses and rebar above. The children's faces redden and shine, and tiny veins stick out on their necks. Music is their God gift; the black cloud of sin dissipates, the Devil in exile.

Father Ernst bangs the table, triumphant. "This is the Word and the Law. Time for Doctrine Studies, children," he says, dismissing them with a wave.

"Cousin Hannah, a word." He strides to unlock his chamber door and she comes to him. She comes with her sly smile and small, hungry hands.

CHAPTER 3

Susan watches Ernst, back to his usual commanding self. Hannah—
the swagger of being chosen, of holding the man's desire. The girl
always struts. Shoulders back and small chest raised, she thrusts
from the hips as though wading upstream.

Once, about a year ago, midway through Devotions, Hannah
faltered. Air whooshed out of her, dragging an animal moan.
She gathered her skirt and raised it high, showing grey socks,
down-covered stick-shins, the large knobs of her knees, her worm-
white thighs. Female parts exposed before the disbelieving circle.
Her eyes rolled. Her head and shoulders shook. Foam spotted her
lips. She thrust herself, gurgling and grotesque, toward Cousin
Paul. Susan was the first to react, shouting, "Hie thee!" The boy ran.
Susan and Rebekah dragged Hannah to the infirmary where she
convulsed, then lay still, the rage come upon her and gone at last,
Satan having rushed right through. How pale, how queerly quiet
she was for days until Susan bade Father visit. It shocked her that
he would mount a girl in that condition. But hymns were sung for
their union. Hannah was draped in the marriage shawl and thusly
named a wife. Ernst has scarcely bothered Susan or Rebekah since
that night, to their private relief.

"Shoo," Susan says to the children. She proceeds to wipe the
long table, the benches, and then to fetch the straw broom from the
kitchen corner to sweep the floor. Rebekah makes a half-hearted

gesture to take the broom and Susan clucks her teeth. May as well keep at her interminable sewing. No one else is so adept. Other than working her quilt incessantly, as she's done for weeks now, Rebekah's been little use all day. Ruth also mopes, now that Paul is gone. It's a disgrace.

Susan begins on the far side nearest Father's chambers, sweeping in long strokes away from the walls, piling the debris right in front of his door. She leans heavily against it while she stoops to brush the dirt into the dustpan. Inside, the girl murmurs something, her fairy laugh teases. That insipid voice. How Ernst can take it, Susan doesn't know. There. His chest-deep rumble, a kind of sigh. Susan pictures him: eyes closing, mouth opening, the pink of his tongue parting the wiry moustache. It has been a very long time, but Susan remembers the prickle and itch of that long beard against her skin. She would rash up, especially along the neck, and those hives had their own telling, their own kind of pride and shame.

For a while she herself was his first choice, despite her clubfoot, her bent back. She was a seventeen-year-old runaway when Memaw Ruth and Mother Deborah, God rest them both, found her hiding out in the gas station restroom attached to the diner on I-75, trying to ditch her lunch bill. They were driving back from the city, had stopped to fill the tank, and if it weren't for Deborah's delicate stomach, they might have never met. God Himself only knows what would have become of Susan. How kind was Memaw Ruth, holding Susan's dirty chin between those soft fingers and seeing her, seeing everything—the backpack, the hurts, the fear in her eyes.

"Come," she had said. "We have a farm. You'll work for your bed and board, but only doing what suits you, no more and no less than anyone else. You'll come to church. But you can leave whenever you like. I promise, you'll be let alone." As she spoke, Memaw Ruth wetted a paper towel and wiped at Susan's face, the grime and sweat, the dried ketchup at the corners of her mouth.

A peculiar sensation—Susan's insides heating and shifting unexpectedly, the swell catching at the back of her throat. At first she suspected the meatloaf sandwich was off, that she would pay in other ways for thieving. But this unfamiliar feeling did not vanish in the coming weeks. It would subside then flourish again whenever Memaw was near. Susan never spoke that first day, only nodded, and waited while the women conferred with a solemn, handsome man. It was settled. Father Ernst paid Susan's lunch bill, and she climbed into the back of their Chevrolet pickup and off they drove, to her new home.

Still sweeping, Susan fans out toward the table. The children are down in the empty bunkroom, now a classroom, their voices contained by the concrete walls. She likes being alone; it's rare. More space to think and not think without their fuss. She has to go back near Father Ernst's door for the dustpan, and as she bends she hears sounds like a bird cooing, a rising insistence, that babydoll voice gasping, and Ernst extolling great effort, grunting, grunting, and a strangled shout: release.

Susan has heard this all before, of course. Ernst has become louder but is otherwise much the same. It's Hannah that confuses her—what is the point in pretending? The girl couldn't really like it, could she?

Susan didn't mind obliging Father Ernst. He had been good to her. But she would not say she ever looked forward to it. Memaw was the one she loved. Memaw gifted her orthopaedic shoes to help correct her damaged foot. Urged her to take calcium supplements and to practice spine-strengthening exercises. In the months following her arrival, Susan wore the heavy shoes on sunset walks along the ridge—a halting gait, the right always leading, the left dragging behind, hip resisting. Each step buoyed and lured her with apparitions of an unexpected future—Susan, tall and slim; Susan dancing with grace; Susan, pretty and friendly and liked. Normal, at last.

Father Ernst began to appear regularly, often sitting beneath a gnarled apple tree that overlooked the valley, as good a place as any for her to rest and talk. Later, he nestled close and held her hand while he explained about his marriages, how the wives worked together and how the children were a Holy tribe, belonging to all of them equally. Later still, he talked about their vows and, eventually, one night he asked her to lie back and give herself to him the way his other wives did. Susan did so, silent, on the least lumpy piece of ground. She never mentioned her personal history of this same thing, never told him that she had been lying down for men since she was a child. Lying down, she had learned, was better than being knocked down. Her permanent injuries evidence.

"I had to go slow with you," Ernst once said. "I knew some of your great sorrows from that life before the Farm, and I wanted you to decide."

Had he truly known? If so, how dare he approach her at all?

Susan sweeps with great momentum; she is raising the dust. Come to think on it, had she actually decided? Or had she merely permitted it—a different thing entirely.

At the time, Memaw Ruth had her suspicions and oh so gently broached the topic. They were rolling pie pastry in the big kitchen, and Susan was nervous. Would Memaw be cross or jealous? Would their friendship be affected? She didn't notice the tension creeping into her shoulders, but Memaw Ruth observed the stretch of the dough, the way Susan flattened one side into the counter without mercy, tearing it. Ruth's lightly floured hand rested on Susan's and she stopped working the pin.

"I don't begrudge Ernst taking another wife," she said. "I can't bear more children, and we've only the one daughter, my own Ruth. But I promised you'd be left alone here. I worry this is not what you truly want."

Susan said, "Oh, it don't bother me much."

And Memaw said, "Susan, it should feel better than that, it should feel welcome."

Susan gaped in amazement. "Why would any woman welcome it?"

"Why not?"

"Well, the apples are bad for my backside. But pinecones, that's where I draw the line."

Memaw stared, uncomprehending.

"Father Ernst took me in the orchard until I asked otherwise, on account of the apples staining my dress. Now he likes it in the forest under the pines, but those cones hurt like a son of a gun."

Memaw coughed and smiled behind her hand, then tossed some flour at Susan, who blinked rapidly and barked a strange laugh. They looked away. Looked back. And they began to snort and hoot, and when one finally wound down, the other would crumble and the laughing start up again.

How she loved Memaw, like no other.

Despite that odious wifely chore, if anyone ever bothered to ask—and no one had, not before and not since Memaw—Susan knows what she would say. That Ernst was the first man to ask her opinion about anything. The first man to look her in the eyes and speak in quiet full sentences. The first to give and not just take, take. It counted for something. It counted for a lot.

CHAPTER 4

Paul crouches on the rise camouflaging the bunker entrance, rifle across his knees, facing what's left of the compound. He runs his hand the length of the barrel, reacquainting himself with the Ruger Scout. It resides in Father Ernst's locked chamber except for when Paul comes topside to hunt, same with the ammo. Wind pelts hot sand that stings his back through the coveralls. Even with the Desert Locust goggles, his eyes water from brightness. He's a blind mole after being underground. He stays put a long time, adjusting. So long that his feet sink, and a warm ledge drifts against him. He is part of the landscape, hot and white. If he falls asleep, he'll be buried alive.

He slithers several feet to a gnarled shrub—big sagebrush—and curls in its fragrant shade. The marked temperature difference stays the perspiration that has begun to bead and run along his hairline under the rubber gas mask. He lifts binoculars and scans. It's as though the entire farm has sunk, like Atlantis, since his last forage. Sand has drifted to banks that hug and obscure piles of debris, sloping and cresting, catching the sun. Like a photograph he once saw of the Arctic—only that was snow and glacial ice reflecting radiant light.

Had it faced any other direction, the bunker entrance would be buried, the family inhumed. He should find a shovel. Keep it inside the first set of doors, in case.

Eventually, he picks out the military fence lining their property.

Homeland Security tape, pulled loose and knotted, flaps in places along the barricades, the only detectable movement. No guards. No soldiers. The outpost tower that the military constructed after the Standoff looks abandoned, tilted, a cenotaph leaning toward its own grave. The church is more or less the same—gutted. Blackened from a long-ago fire. The collapsed steeple blanketed. The main barn's skeleton languishes; granary gone, roof caved in, main supports lurching toward one another like the ribs of an ancient whale. Deborah's clapboard is gone, same with Mary's. The original farmhouse, Memaw's A-frame, is mostly levelled. A remnant of chimney reaches up from the rubble, a desperate brick hand. Cabins are brick piles and charred logs. Those buildings were picked clean a long time ago. All save the kill house which endures, squat and disquieting, at the edge of sand-whipped fields, gone to seed. He can take cover inside until evening, when the temperature drops. Its thick cement walls protect from heat. Once in, he'll lose his sight advantage—no windows.

Tonight he must venture across the sands. A vulture circles far off, near the forest. Trees mean water, soil, shade. But anyone could be camping out, making a pit stop. Humans are the thing to worry about now, especially revolutionaries, members of the rumoured underground coalition. They'd kill him on sight. Cousin Thomas spied several on missions, even tracked them through the forest. Likely how he met his demise. So Paul carries a knife and the long-range Ruger Scout. The magazine holds ten rounds, and there's the box of ammo in his pocket. Gunshots will attract attention; there's no telling who or what else would come sniffing around, but he can't risk an injury fighting close. He'll go either to that wooded glade, the outline of which he can discern through the glass, or veering slightly north, to the white cliff beyond. There he'd be able to survey: settlements, agriculture, military activity. Less chance of food, but he'd be able to find out what, if anything, is going on.

Little Jericho River follows the base of the white cliff, winding its way to a deep pond where he and his father used to fish. Twilight used to bring all manner of animals to drink. He and his dad would harvest cattails. They boiled the rhizomes and stems, and steamed the leaves that tasted a lot like spinach. In early summer, they'd break off the spikes and eat them like corn-on-the-cob. Plus spindly stalks of wild asparagus, plantain, lamb's quarter, and the curled tips of bracken—all delicious when steamed and sprinkled with salt. Farther in, a small marsh was home to a tiny, perfectly balanced universe: frogs on lily pads, snapping turtles, and long-legged hunting birds poised to strike. But on his last expedition, the river was dangerously low, dried to mud bed in places. Most of the plants gone. He had to dig in the outside bend like a burro to drink, and although the water that pooled through into the hole was naturally filtered by the soil, it was likely tainted with bacteria or microbes. He didn't have any more purification tablets and hadn't made a fire to boil the water before drinking. Probably what made him sick. He'd been too weak to climb the escarpment and had barely found enough food to sustain himself. Fish bellies broke the surface of the oversized puddle—all that remained of the lake. Hardpan extended beyond;

he was able to scrape the salt crust to fill a sack, but it's a wonder he made it back to the bunker.

He might survive the trek to the cliff, but he'll die if there is nothing left to nourish him.

Or—and this is a wild thought—he could head in the opposite direction, to the city. Follow the highway. He could find the authorities, whoever is left. No doubt Father Ernst is still wanted for domestic terrorism, instigating the Standoff. Would they believe a scrawny young man? They might arrest or kill him instead, and then what? The Family would die. He pictures a SWAT team bursting the bunker doors, jogging the tunnel, surprising them mid-prayer. Shooting the whole lot. Children and women. His sister, whom he is sworn to protect. His lover.

Drought has worsened, certainly. That began long before they went to ground. He remembers men hunched around the table, maps spread, *Farmer's Almanac* so thumbed it could stand open on any page, tracing the desert spread with calloused fingers. California, New Mexico, Texas, Utah, and Arizona—those were a given. The central and southern plains succumbed as well; the Big Drought ravaged most of the country. Reservoirs were low, even in the Northeast, and precipitation fell so far below normal each season it was difficult to measure.

"Why now?" some asked.

"God, of course," Father Ernst said. "God is punishing the heathens."

Paul's dad said, "Greenhouse gases, industry, climate change."

When Father Ernst took exception, he argued. "Ernst, they're draining the water table to irrigate. Sucking it right out from underneath themselves. Landslides, sinkholes. Remember Florida?"

The men removed their hats and stood a moment in silence. Paul followed suit. "Remember Florida," they said. "Remember New Orleans."

"It was only a matter of time. It's science, not God's vengeance."

Father Ernst ended the meeting and told Paul to wait for his dad outside while the others dispersed. He could hear them yelling, even through the thick door, the closed windows. Nobody else contradicted their leader, ever.

His dad, later called a traitor. Ritually unnamed.

Paul's dad could do anything. Start fire without matches. Find water, treat it. Harvest edible weeds. Read the constellations to find his way. He'd given Paul the Ruger, taught him how to use it. Taught Ruth how to survive too, although she was pretty young. Paul keeps at her, quizzing her skills. What would their dad do, search for information or search for food? He can almost hear his dad's voice. *Head to the forest. No use learning anything if it'll just get you killed.*

Thinking in the past can get you killed too.

Paul loosens his fists and warm sand streams through his fingers like a girl's long, unknotted hair, until his hands come up empty.

CHAPTER 5

Sometimes Rebekah sees the future. It is jagged, frequently brutish, and she herself is never there. Things that have already come to pass: she envisioned the twins turning in Susan's rough hands, wiped clean of afterbirth. This well before Susan even fell pregnant. Saw Mother Deborah covered in the cancerous sores that, a decade later, consumed her. Dreamed Paul trembling, lips parted, aching for her, months before their first kiss.

Things that may or may not have come to pass: a forest engulfed in flames, the white cliff swarmed by military, a thousand birds falling from the sky at once, their stiff little legs grasping at nothing. How can she know if these pictures are true? She's been buried for years. One sequence comes to her again and again: a girl running and running and then tripping, falling, captured by terrifying men. With this, she wakes drenched in sweat. Who is the girl? She never sees her face, only the back of her small figure, hair flying out behind her, bare feet pounding the burning sand.

Most recently, she is transfixed by a horrific tableau that she stitches into the quilt's centrepiece each evening, trance-like, until she cannot keep her eyes open. She shows it to no one. She cannot shake its importance: it is a message, certainly. But for whom? It feels connected to her beloved older sister, long since exiled. Certainly not Father Ernst or Susan. If either of them sees it, Rebekah will get much more than a whipping. She will suffer and burn.

Bedtime, at long last. Rebekah prays she will not wake on the morrow.

Since childhood, this has been a sanctuary: her cotton-swabbed dream world where all the mothers retire in glory and their dead babies sleep unperturbed. White and fuzzy filters for this softly padded place of pale blue light. It smells good here and voices ring like bells, clear and bright. She hears them, and though they do not speak any kind of language, she knows their meaning. She is transported, comforted. Elsewhere.

She is in a sun-drenched meadow.

She is up a gnarled oak.

She is swinging a metal pail on the way to milking.

Lo, she is in her lover's arms, nesting in the orchard on the southwest ridge, watching the sunset.

Then Susan's scraping voice: "Hie thee!" A thump on her cot.

Rebekah's eyelids twitch, and she grips her rough blanket, trying to claw her way back to that wonderful place. It eludes her. Her eyes open to the dismal room, and she groans. Finally, she sits up on the thin mattress and coils squeak in the bedframe. The horror of another dank day. The indignities of bunker living, of Father Ernst's putrid chamber.

"Good morning, Mother Rebekah," sings Leah.

"Good morning," say the twins, Rachel and Helen, their uncanny movements mirroring one another.

"Morning," she whispers.

Ruth watches her with haunted eyes—now what has she gone

and done?—and Susan's sharp gaze follows Rebekah as she slowly stands and shakes the bed sheets out, as she straightens and folds and turns them back carefully, just as she does every day.

Rebekah hangs her nightdress and cap. She dons a cotton dress over the full slip she no longer removes. With her back to the others she rests a hand on her hard belly, hoping. Nothing, at first. Then, there it is: a slow turning inside. How could it be? Rebekah wipes at her eyes. How could he leave? She ties an apron high on her waist with a sharp tug and follows Susan, the grim reaper herself, out to the galley kitchen.

Breakfast, such as it is. Susan rings the bell. Spoons knock against bowls and then the sweeping, mopping, the washing up. Tending the children, the pretty, clinging children. They love her, a small mercy. Lunch, there is hardly anything. Then more sweeping, more washing up. Minutes are hours, hours an eternity. She'll do laundry if there's water. Tidy the bedrooms if not. Her body is pulled toward the infirmary; she pretends it wants dusting. Rebekah catches her reflection in the medicine cabinet door. She is all angles and shadow. *Who am I?* Inside, the shelves are nearly bare. A bit of gauze and expired ointment, a thermometer. Taped to the underside of the bottom shelf are the last three pain pills, believed by the Family to be long since gone. She takes one, cuts it in half with a razor blade. Swallows a piece dry. Dabs at the chalky crumbs with fingertips that she licks greedily. She hides the other bits with the blade and secures the tape back in place. How else can she get through these days?

Now, supper. She has her strength back. It hardly matters that she must wash the dreaded dishes, again. And all that praying. Praying he'll return soon. Praying for swift retribution, that's what. For an end to their suffering.

After dinner, the lighting is so poor she can hardly manage the fine work on the quilt, much of which is by hand. The ancient treadle machine, powered by foot, finishes the longer seams. She will use it to bind the edges, sealing all three layers together. Despite severe restrictions—fabrics co-opted from raggedy old clothes, limited embroidery floss, and threads in strange colours—Rebekah is pleased with her stack of finished bold blocks. She is almost done connecting the top layer: double diamonds for the border squares, pinwheels as the main background, yards of gunmetal sashings, and the beautiful appliqué corner blocks—painstaking portraits of the first four mothers. The central image, her secret mosaic, demands meticulous paper piecing. It's a variation on the Ascension, a pattern she designed last year, and her best work to date.

She asked Ruth to help, but the girl is all thumbs and her sloppy quarter-inch seams had to be ripped out and redone twice. Ruth is better with her knife than with a needle. So much for the romantic notion of an underground quilting bee. It could have helped pass the time, given them a shared sense of purpose. But the magic, the profound sense of satisfaction, was lost on the others.

"Memaw always said that a proper quilt requires the precise convergence of mathematics, logic, and creativity," said Rebekah. "A true masterpiece holds, in addition, an unnameable element, its own uncommon spirit."

"I hate sewing," said Ruth.

"It's not just sewing, it's an archive. A history, if you know how to look."

"Arthritis," said Susan, flexing and curling her fingers.

Alas. Rebekah inters herself in the work, busies her hands, her mind. She transposes her mystical images into rough sketches and animates them with fabric. She measures, marks with pencil, pins, and finally, commits to precision snipping with the long-handled scissors. A dismembered dress piles at her feet. Sleeves, now cut to pieces. Bodice, ripped open on the seams. And the labour-intensive reparations: stitching all these forlorn bits back together into one cohesive work of art. Functional—and infused with her very essence.

Rebekah's only other solace is her stolen moments with the boy. Grimy, sweet skin and lips as soft as a girl's. A terrible chance to take. They are doomed, but she can't, she won't stop. With him topside, it's pure misery. And what if he doesn't return? He barely survived his last forage. She can't endure this dreary place without Paul.

She will not.

Until his return, there is the quilt to finish—an utter compulsion—and the dreamtime that consumes more of her, sleeping and awake. She can travel there almost on whim. The pills help. Sitting quietly in the hard fast, for example, or during Reflections, or even at table, her body still inhabits the Great Hall but her mind may be full of beauteous, otherworldly creatures. God's garden—the Family speaks of it endlessly—is where Rebekah travels when she's between worlds, she's sure of it. And any moment that she is permitted to sit, even working her needle and thread, she can fly there swiftly in secret and lose herself in her world of forest and fairy and infinite possibility.

CHAPTER 6

Ruth stifles a yawn. Cousin Silas paces in front of the children, just like Father Ernst, but it doesn't have the same mesmerizing effect; they can't sit still. He taps the front of the classroom with a long ruler. Nothing. He taps Leah, the littlest, on her head.

"That's enough," he says. "If you long to speak, tell the story of our Great Standoff, of our Martyrs' Sacrifice and our Exodus, of our going to ground. Elsewise, shut your mouths."

He turns and sweeps his arms, also like Father Ernst, and in his most dramatic voice says, "Humble, we are, though ever despised by godless fornicators for our faith. This is our legacy, your inheritance, more precious than gold or weapons or water."

"We shall never starve so long as we hold history in our mouths," the children reply.

"Very good," says Silas. "So ends our Lesson on the Doctrine." He shoos them away with a flick of his wrists, another gesture copied from Father Ernst.

Will he ever command a room like Father? Ruth sincerely doubts it. Yet he is driven to try, starved for attention of almost any kind. With Paul topside, he's got even less competition. From pity she says, "You done a good job, Silas."

"Really?" His face warms with pleasure. "Tomorrow I'll review our Martyrs' Pledge. What do you think about that?"

But Ruth is gone already; not even her shadow lingers.

Ruth corrals the girls back to their room where the twins solemnly brush and braid one another's hair. She sits on her cot, entranced, watching Helen and Rachel. Their daily grooming has become an elaborate, private ritual, wordless, yet language flows through their bodies in the acts of looking and touching and knowing. In the knotting of hair, spells are cast.

"Do mine?" says little Leah, climbing onto Ruth's lap waving a comb.

The twins stop and stare until Leah squirms.

"I never get to say nothing," says Leah.

The older girls resume their mirrored dance, twining and plaiting and tying with ribbons.

Ruth begins to work through Leah's thin curls. The comb snags and Leah whimpers. "Sorry. We'll get those out, don't worry. At least there's no lice." Loose strands gather and, much like Ruth's own, fall out in tufts. Ruth collects them in a separate pile that she worries between her fingers. Bald patches are beginning to show on the child, which Rebekah once said is on account of not getting enough protein.

"There," says Ruth when she's done, and pets Leah's hand-me-down sweater. Its one Ruth also wore many years ago, though the colours are faded and the sleeves are stretched to fraying. Leah's fingers trace Ruth's face and settle on her lips.

"Where's Mother Hannah?" asks Leah. "Is she my mother?"

"All of the mothers are your mother," says Ruth, pretending to chomp those fingertips. "You know that."

"Yes, but do I belong more to one?"

"Maybe, but not Hannah."

"Then who?"

Helen says, "You belong to God."

Rachel and Helen climb onto the bed beside Ruth and Leah. Their downy limbs hook together at the knees and elbows to huddle for warmth. "Leah come out of Mother Rebekah," says Rachel.

"Mother Rebekah?" says Leah.

In that instant, Rebekah appears in the doorway. Gaunt in the shadows, sections of the quilt she's been working on folded neatly over one arm.

Leah reaches out for her. "You're my tummy mother?"

Rebekah covers her face with the quilt and gasps. She's crying. Just as suddenly, she disappears back into the dark hallway.

Ruth clears her throat but says nothing. What on earth is wrong with Rebekah?

"Nobody likes me," pouts Leah.

"Don't be silly. I like you. Now it's bedtime." Ruth nudges Leah back to her cot. She whisks her out of her patched dress and rummages in the underbed storage trunk to find a clean nightshirt.

Leah rubs her rounded belly. "What about them? Who's their mother?"

"Mother Susan bore the twins," says Ruth. She shakes loose a nightshirt and helps Leah change into it.

The twins strip out of their dresses. "*Susan*," one says. "That old humpback don't even like us. Why can't we have Hannah? Hannah's pretty."

"Hmph. Hannah's not old enough," says Ruth.

The twins fold and tuck their clothes away. The nightdresses, all cut from the same pattern, are greying and translucent with wear. When the girls file out the door and down the hall they drift like little ghosts.

"Toilet, then wash hands and faces, then brush teeth," says Ruth. In the latrine she pushes the grey-water bucket closer to the sinks. She is already tiring despite the mouthful of meat. Ruth's hunger wakes, as though the bite they had for supper—which seems like days ago rather than an hour or two—only made it worse. Tomorrow they're back to plain oats with a pinch of salt to help it go down. Not even a shake of spice or sugar or dried fruit. Only God knows when Paul will return or what he'll bring.

Three sets of eyes stare at her. Helen whispers to Rachel.

"What?" says Ruth.

"Who're you talking to?" asks Leah.

"No one." Was she speaking out loud?

Normally, Rebekah puts the girls to bed. Susan, on the other hand, will sweep the Hall three times over to avoid it. And Hannah is too good for either chore. She and Father Ernst practice begetting quite a lot—the muffled sounds of which send Ruth shamed and curious to her own bunk—so Hannah is never around at bedtime. Hannah wants to conceive like she wants to win at checkers, but it doesn't come easy. Mother Susan says none of them has got enough on their bones; it'd take a miracle. She should know. She birthed a dozen in her time, now mostly departed by one means or another.

And as Rebekah whispered so strangely the other day, "What will we do with another baby?"

"You're mumbling again," says Leah.

"What—"

"Who're you talking to?"

"Oh," says Ruth. "Nobody."

Back in the bunkroom, Ruth tucks the girls in bed. Rebekah is still missing, who knows where—not that there are many places to hide. She must be elbow deep in her quilt pattern to not say goodnight.

"Tell us a story?" says Helen. "Tell about the Martyrs."

Ruth sits on the edge of Leah's bed and rubs her hands to warm them. It wasn't that long ago she herself was being put to bed, most often by Rebekah, who whispered stories from a book she knew almost by heart, a forbidden book of tales she had been given by the nameless sister. It had been secreted to their home and kept hidden in Mother Deborah's topside house for years. "I'd have snuck it into the bunker had I known how long we'd be here," Rebekah once said in private. "I miss the pictures."

Ruth says, "Here's a story told to me long ago. It's secret. Can you keep a secret?"

"I can," says Leah.

"She cannot," says Helen. "She blabs everything, doesn't she, Rachel?"

Rachel nods and Leah says, "I can so!"

Ruth says, "There'll be no story if you don't shut it. This story—that we will not mention outside this room—is about twelve princesses, all sisters."

"What's a princess?" asks Leah.

"A king's daughter," says Ruth.

"You mean Jesus Christ, King of Kings?" That's Helen.

"No. Just a regular king, a person in charge of a country."

"Like Father Ernst?"

"Kind of. Are you done?"

"Fine," says Helen.

"The king was upset because each morning when he unlocked the bedroom his twelve daughters shared, they were exhausted. It was as though they had not slept, and each morning their shoes were worn down to nothing, as though they had been walking or running or even dancing all night long. Each day, twelve new pairs of shoes had to be made for their feet, and the following morning it was always the same; the girls were tired and sore and bad-tempered, and the soles of their shoes were worn right through."

"I didn't know shoes had souls," says Rachel.

"The other kind," says Ruth, and pulls off her slipper. She shows them the thinned-out bottom bit.

"The king wanted to solve this mystery, so he announced a contest all across the land," Ruth continues. "If anyone could discover what the daughters were doing at night, he would be given jewels and a feast and a castle and a dog and a horse and a beautiful sword and pie and also he could marry any of the daughters that he liked. But if he failed to solve the mystery, he would be brought into the

Great Hall of the palace and he would have his head cut right off and that would be the end of him."

"Ooh." Rachel draws back against the pillow, frightened.

"How did they cut off the head?" says Leah. "With scissors?"

"No. Probably a sword or a machete. Maybe an axe. They'd make him kneel over a bucket, so the man's head would land inside and make less mess for the old woman who had to mop."

Rachel says, "Yuck."

Leah says, "I'm scared."

"Listen," says Ruth. "If you don't like this one, I can tell you about a winged dragon that breathes fire—"

"The Devil!" says Helen.

"Or a toad that becomes a handsome man when a girl kisses it, or one about an old gnome who turns hay into gold thread."

"Cousin Ruth, what's the meaning of this?" Susan is leaning in the doorway behind Ruth. How long has she been there? "What stories are these?"

Ruth opens her mouth, then shuts it.

"That is not the Doctrine, nor the history of our great Martyrs. Answer me."

"Only a dream I had," says Ruth.

"Sorcery and lies," says Susan. "Be zealous, therefore, and repent!"

"I'm sorry," says Ruth and ducks her head.

"Unclean beasts, fornication, false prophets," says Susan, advancing on Ruth. She strikes her about the head and shoulders, shouting. "'Behold, he cometh with clouds: and all kindred of the earth shall wail because of him.' Get, and do not show yourself again tonight! The Devil has had at you."

Ruth is up and out the door, down the hall. The Great Hall is empty, just Silas peddling, slow and steady on the stationary bike. He waves. The tunnel door is unlatched and Ruth slides it open, closes it behind her. It's dark and cold, colder than the bunker main rooms. She strides halfway and curls up at the cairn.

"Father in Heaven forgive me," she says.

A whipping, most likely. She'll have to reflect tomorrow, take her licks from Father Ernst. Rebekah, too, if he finds out about the book.

Paul told her to check on Rebekah, right before he left. And to stay out of trouble. She'd done neither. Him gone a few hours, and already Ruth is in for it.

"Forgive me, Paul," she says.

Where could Rebekah even be? Ruth peers down the black tunnel. Could she be haunting the Mission Pole ladder, waiting on Paul's return? A stillness. Silence. Ruth would know if someone was down there. Wouldn't she?

She steadies her nerves. Father will dole it out, and she can take it. Reflections is rougher on the mothers, everyone knows. She can't bear to see Rebekah suffer, especially now in her great distress. For when Father Ernst must punish a mother, it's a terrible, terrible thing.

CHAPTER 7

The temperature dips and relents. Paul wipes sweat from his forehead and lowers the shovel. He's dug a hole about a foot deep and placed a large tin can at the bottom. Then he filled the hole around the can with scrub vegetation pulled from the sand. Now he places a piece of clear plastic over top to trap the condensation. He buries the edges, lines them with stones to hold the can and the plastic tarp in place. Last, he sets a palm-sized rock in the centre, above the can, so the drops will run and collect in the tin. By the time he returns from the forest, it should be full of drinkable water. Next, he wraps a plastic bag around a leafy low branch of an ash tree, then duct tapes it securely. This, too, should produce water for drinking. He'd set more water traps but he didn't bring any more plastic sheeting with him, and even this light activity is draining. Paul needs to rest.

If he finds thistles and removes the thorns, he can chew on the stalks to relieve thirst. Or cut into a wild grapevine with his sharp knife—that will produce actual water. Survival tips ricochet through his mind, but he must focus. Mistakes happen when you're jumpy, and even one error can be fatal. The rule of three—Paul's father drilled it into them: *three weeks without food, three days without water, but even three hours of exposure can be fatal.*

Paul lies on the kill-house floor beside the Ruger Scout, sleeping and waking in starts. Light dulls in the cracks around the door when he opens his eyes. And when he closes them, his dreams ooze blood memories, offal, the terror of animals come to slaughter. That final culling was mythic. Hens, turkeys, grouse, partridge, one after the other, killed on this very stone, plucked clean and cut up and frozen before they went to ground. A dozen pigs. Three cows. It took days, around the clock. They were to run off the dogs or shoot them, drown the cats. If even one loyal or desperate animal was observed on their scent trail, it could give the bunker away. It was a massacre.

"Forgive us," Paul whispers to the shadows. But why should they?

Father Ernst sold the horses except for their one great stallion that he gifted, along with the donkey, to a neighbouring farmer. Advance apology. The horse cost a lot, but not even close to meeting the damages of an invading military, the inconvenience of cross-examinations and government suspicions.

Paul sets the magazine upright on the floor beside him. He holds the base of the top cartridge down with one hand and slips the next cartridge into the magazine with the other, and so on, until it is full. Ten rounds. A few bullets left in the box. Hopefully he will not have to reload out in the open. He polishes the grey laminate with a cloth, wipes the custom eighteen-inch barrel. It is smooth and comforting under his fingers. His dad chose the longer barrel without a flash suppressor. It was too large for him to carry easily when he was a child, but Paul has grown into it. He fits the magazine into the opening and slaps it in place, flicks the safety on and slings the Ruger over his shoulder. It is time.

He is cautious opening the door, leaving the shelter. The light is softer, glare reduced. The wind has dropped off.

Walking parallel to the old highway for now, he's able to set a good pace. He peers through the binoculars at intervals. Nothing. He finds a good stick about two feet long, as thick as his wrist and straight. Heavy. He lifts it, practices swinging it. He throws it, keeps walking and bends to pick it up as he passes it. Throws again. And again. He targets scruff; the stick lands true. Then an abandoned cola can, which he pockets. If he runs out of matches, he can angle the bottom of the can to reflect sunlight and set dry tinder alight. Something else his dad taught him. Paul walks on, using the stick to steady himself, measuring progress not by time, which is deceptive, but by footfalls. Two thousand steps per mile, he guesses, at reduced speed because of his weakened condition. He counts as high as he can before losing focus, fudging numbers. He starts over. After a time he gives up. He lets the rhythm of his feet on the dry, cracked ground guide him.

Soon he is far enough away from the compound that he cannot see the dilapidated barn, the burned church, unaided. Sand behind him, sand ahead. Used to be fields—flatlands interrupted by the occasional silo, water tower, and endless telephone poles like giant crucifixes lining the highway, reminding him always of Christ's great sorrow. Now the poles careen, drunks holding each other up. Failing that, they topple flat. Miles of wire that once hummed and sliced the great sky dip and pool on the sand like black snakes.

Paul shivers. Serpents. They always represent the devil in

Scriptures and in Father Ernst's sermons. As a small boy, Paul pictured them, wicked and lying in wait. Terrifying. He imagined them everywhere—inching along tree branches, coiled beneath rocks, looped with irrigation tubing, or hiding in the darkest crooks of the barn. Poised to attack, nefarious and ripe with poison. It got so bad Paul refused to go out after dark, refused to do his chores or to use the outhouse alone. He couldn't be reasoned with.

It was his mother, big with child, who took him by the hand to the forest. She pointed out the various nests of birds and small animals. He recognized many tracks already, despite being so young. Finally, she showed him small holes disguised by long grass or trailing plants, not unlike the tunnels made by moles. "Inside here is another family trying to survive," she said. "God made everything in His image, so how can snakes be bad? They deserve a life too."

Paul recalls the quiet tremor of her voice. Unlike Father Ernst, she didn't need to shout to be heard. Her face, framed by curling hair, was kind. Beautiful, he supposed. She died giving birth to Ruth not long after that day. To honour her memory, he works hard to staunch the old fears. He doesn't think about her often, but once in a long while, when he least expects it, an image of her appears like a knife in his most tender parts, gutting him.

Paul stops in the hot sand. His shoulders stoop from fatigue and from this sorrowful cloak—memory. He leans on his stick. Peering backward, his strange three-legged tracks diminish toward the horizon. Anyone discovering them will assume he's old or seriously injured, using a walking stick. They'll ignore him altogether or at least underestimate him in a fight. Perspiration runs slick down his back, along the sides of his face. He must slow down and steady his breath. Sweating is the fastest way to dehydrate, worse than running out of drinking water. He pushes the gas mask up, and the cooling wind dries his face. The air seems clear, clean. Still, there are few mosquitoes, and he's hardly seen a bird in his travels: could be chemicals on the wind, driving them away, killing them. He digs a few inches down in the sand to where it is cooler and finds a pebble, pops it in his mouth. He sucks on it, keeping his lips pressed closed, to conserve water and stave off the feeling of thirst.

Paul surveys the horizon. Another long stretch done. He examines the outline of scrub in the glass ahead—a good place to rest. There, the land will be interrupted by plant life more frequently, and the heat of the day will feel less drying on his parched skin. Maybe there'll be some yucca he can dig up. The roots are nutritious. Memaw used to use the pointy tips as needles to suture wounds on their camp-outs. When she rubbed the fresh leaves underwater, it produced a frothy green soap. Dry yucca leaves could be twined together to make a kind of ropey kindling. These things alone will improve bunker life. And so Paul lowers the mask. He keeps on.

Behind him, the sun begins its true descent. The sky brightens, a fireball burst: Armageddon. He sways, staring. The children have never seen a sunset. Never seen the sun. How could he begin to describe it? These colours don't have names. And there are no reference points in the bunker, only greys, dirty whites, faded pastels. Sombre trousers and jackets for the boys. The brightest things come, always, from Rebekah's fingertips, her spools of thread, a nearly forgotten rainbow that she coaxes in and out, drawing scenes with her deft needle.

Rebekah. If he can give her one thing it will be this sunset—not this exact one, but another glorious blaze, and he will sit beside her all night as darkness falls thickly and the stars blink into being, one by one by one. Surely this is where God lives, out in the open, in the black skies of midnight under the luminous moon that waxes and wanes in it's own secretive cycle. He can feel her beside him now—the anticipating shiver, the pull of her long hair when he fingers apart her braid. The silent shock of skin on skin. The wonder of her lips, kissing him. For once, under God's sky, they could live without the brooding fear of discovery gnawing away their small joy.

CHAPTER 8

Father Ernst bangs the gavel. "Sin is a topside virus that spreads if not cured or cast out. Even in God's chosen family, sin can enter the refuge and take root. Let us dig it out. Let us reveal our temptations and, in so doing, let us cleanse our hearts and our minds."

"We cleanse them in gladness and rejoice," says the Family.

"Who among us bears a shame burden?"

From habit, Father Ernst looks for Cousin Paul. But Paul's grim smile, the dark glitter of his eyes, is not here to provoke. Hannah stares into her empty lap. All around the table the children are blank as bunker walls, all but Cousin Silas, of course. No doubt he had his hand in the oats barrel again. Little girls fidget. Mother Rebekah stops stitching, holds her breath. Even Susan wipes the creases from her brow, voiding herself of thought, memory. They used to love this—the attention, the redemption. Now it's the same thing every week; furtive eyes, mouths drawn tight, a closing in of bodies and minds.

"No one has the humility to seek forgiveness?" He stares at Ruth until she blushes. She has a wilfulness that wants bridling. "Mother Susan claims our Cousin Ruth has offended—poisoning the impressionable minds of children, straying from Holy Doctrine."

Around the table, chins lift. Shoulders straighten. All save Ruth's.

"Forgive me," she whispers.

They say, "Cousin, we forgive, but only at a cost."

Ruth says, "I see the danger and the folly. I wish not to repeat it."

"Speak. What was this story?"

"It was about twelve sisters whose shoes get worn out each night."

Father Ernst asks, "You made this up?"

She nods, penitent.

He considers Ruth for a moment. She's a terrible liar, red in the cheeks and trembling. In fact, he knows this story from his own childhood.

Father Ernst motions, and the Family, now eager, stands and clasps hands. They sway and hum.

"A proud look and a lying tongue—God hates them, and so do I. This is not your story but a heathen tale from the time before. You forget I am a man of the world. I came along a path of sin and, in my great discouragement with that life, I pledged to start anew. I have heard it all, seen it all, in my tortured youth. Do not think you can fool me, Cousin, for you never can."

Father points to the thin willow in its place on the wall.

"Forgive me, Father. Forgive me, Cousins," Ruth gasps.

She is duly frightened now.

"I can only imagine where you heard this."

The girl blanches. Hands flutter.

"Your traitor birth father, no doubt. All before you came to nestle below in our Holy Sanctum."

Ruth drops her mortified head and covers her face.

How high-strung she is. This, her birth father's shame, this is Ruth's great wound. Father Ernst can see things unfolding even now; how quickly he will make her come to his service. He inhales through his nostrils, counting to lengthen the exhalation. He must not lose control. Ruth is wilful and proud and prone to flights of fancy. She needs discipline, guidance. Yet she is a hard worker and clearly wants his approval. A heady combination—she must be handled just so. It's no coincidence she shall be the seventh.

"Seven Angels with seven vials filled with seven deadly plagues of the tainted earth." This must be God's coded message come to him at last!

It will be his homecoming. He will be reunited with Memaw Ruth in spirit through her lineage in this young body. He knows that now, in the way of knowing God's will; that which is beyond language and reason, a truth that bubbles up from deep within. Perhaps God has been purposefully silent, waiting for him to act. All these other brides were only leading him to this next one, to this final resolution.

"Husband." Hannah nudges him, pouting. She likes to have all of his attention. It's tiresome, not to mention contrary to the Doctrine. She must learn her place. He ignores Hannah's upturned cheek.

He says, "Cousin Ruth, you cannot be trusted with the children. This is a terrible blow to my confidence. You, who are soon to come of age, soon to be my bride."

Beside him, Hannah grimaces. So jealous, this one.

"We await your first blood tide, Cousin. You must know your discipline means everything to the Family. Repeat for me a woman's role."

"A woman's role is modesty and truth," says Ruth. "She is a vessel to hold and care for Father's heart."

"Chastity and vigilance, Cousin. We shall discuss this in private. For now you must seek forgiveness from those whom you've injured. Those present as well as those gone before and the future souls your womb shall one day bear."

Father gestures to the long table, and Ruth crawls beside it on her knees, begging forgiveness from each cousin in turn. Still kneeling, she must beseech the Holy Martyrs. That will pain her. She, who proudly recites the Martyr's Pledge each week for the hard fast. Then she must stand with arms raised and seek forgiveness from the unborn that shall one hopeful day make her womb their home. Her voice quakes. Ruth slumps shame-filled at his feet, palms raised, when he reaches for the whip.

The willow is light in his hand, a conductor's wand, a magician's. Father Ernst bends the tip and lets it fly through the air. A funnel and hiss of wind. The girl flinches. His breath catches high in his chest. If only they were alone. His spine zings with possibility. But the ring of blond heads around her dark one is real. Their mouths gape, faces strain. This is the taut line of Reflections. Shame-burdens unite the Family, and he cannot take that from them now.

Ruth's face is drawn and resolute. Father Ernst hits harder than usual, lands more on each of her palms. He can't help himself. How the willow sings, raising heat inside him with each strike. His hair flops wild, and he shakes it out of his eyes to strike again. Still Ruth does not cry. He wants to push her past this line of control, wants to see the struggle break in her. He needs that vicarious release. Silas, the usual penitent, is too easy, grovelling and snuffling at the first touch; it never feels earned. But Ruth is fierce and proud, just like her brother.

Father Ernst catches himself, a violent spiral churning his guts. And still she is a stone. Her one concession: biting down on her bottom lip until it bleeds. Father Ernst hangs on a precarious cliff, roused by fury. He breathes and paces and tells himself to slow and then, finally, to stop. He replaces the whip on its wall mount. The family is one held breath, shoulders hunched, faces wide and wary, waiting for a familiar settling.

"Let us have the Hymn of Temptation," says Father Ernst in a hoarse voice. Wives and children stir gently and open their mouths to sing.

"Slipped inside our hallowed haven
Satan's morsel of desire
So among us one doth struggle
Tempted by a wicked fire
A golden hook that bears false prophet
Tears the cousin flesh away
So we gather for Devotions
Cousin love has lost her way!"

Father Ernst does not join in. He listens to their harmonies, clasps his trembling hands behind his back, and observes Ruth, colour rising in her cheeks. Otherwise she is a pillar. But whether of the temple or of salt, he does not know. He dares not touch her, not yet. For Ruth shall require strict tutelage as the Seventh. Father Ernst's pulse skips. He cannot wait to begin.

CHAPTER 9

The Chamber of Contemplation is an unloved corner of the bunker. To Ruth, it smells less of body parts and old air than the other rooms. Instead, it sings a song of decay, of mildew and mould with a sulphur cadenza. It's a damp, lonely smell but not an altogether terrible one. Just herself and the cousin board, a narrow pallet to sit or lie upon, and one rough bucket for refuse. Ruth has been here before, of course. Over the years, there have been transgressions and teachings. All cousins need contemplation once in a while. But the chamber seems to have shrunk. Ruth stands with arms and legs wide as a star. Turning slowly, her fingertips brush the dank walls. The gate's metal bars cool her miserable hands. She rests her forehead on them, too.

At least she didn't cry. That's something.

"Stay out of trouble," said Paul. Yet Ruth is well in disgrace. Small comfort he did not witness her shame first hand. He'll hear about it when he returns.

If he returns.

Last time, Paul was gone almost three weeks, long enough to provoke the cousins' grim conclusion. Rebekah commenced the sacred purse, weeping. Father Ernst began training Silas in provisions. Only Ruth refused to believe the worst. She sat sentinel in the cold tunnel and willed his return. She conjured the stoop of his shoulders, his tangled hair. She cast and reeled, retrieved the invisible wire strung between their skulls, their chests and, as she secretly dreamed, mayhap one day their loins. God saw fit to grant her prayer, and a bedraggled Paul reappeared.

Will God hear her prayers now, from this forgotten chamber? Ruth hopes so.

Paul came back a limping shadow, could scarcely activate the code to let the Family know he had returned. He had to be helped down the ladder and led to the infirmary, shaking off fever and sundry topside afflictions. How tenderly Rebekah nursed him, pressing a damp cloth to his brow, petting his curls, and sponging the black soot from his skin. Paul's scent heated the space between them. There were no pain pills left, only two or three aspirin. Rebekah rummaged in the supply drawers—a few squares of gauze, one roll of tape, half a jar of healing ointment, a heinous thick-jellied cream they slathered on to relieve the rattling coughs. A small bit of disinfectant she used to clean his cuts. Bruises had come up, blue spectres on his bare flesh, arms and legs and narrow chest.

He brought contraband—a purple flower with withered leaves drooping from its stalk. Ruth saw it on the cot between them and seized it.

"For me," Ruth said, delighted.

Paul blushed but said nothing.

Rebekah busied herself with refreshing her cloth.

"Used to have them behind the house, near the woodpile," Paul said. "Remember?"

"No," lied Ruth.

"Try," he said.

"That were the past. Hardly matters now."

Paul struggled to sit. "The past *is* who we are. It's partly who we become."

"Must be your fever talking."

Rebekah came then and dabbed at his temples, his brow. His lips.

"Listen," said Paul. "Topside, the ruins is fenced off, quarantined. Guarded, but not as well as last time. Our homes, barns, our fields are all bombed-out. Our church. Even the school is rubble. Hand-painted signs, all over, calling us traitors. *That's* our inheritance. We can hide down here for a hundred years, but it won't change that past. Once we step out of this bunker, we got to accept the truth. All those bones. That's on us."

"You're delirious," Ruth said.

"The Burning Light," whispered Rebekah.

Paul nodded. "We done that. Thousands died because of it."

Ruth said, "'The earth and all who dwell in it shall melt.' Psalms, chapter seventy-five, verse three. We cleansed the earth and cast out demons, as God commanded. See any heathens up there?"

Paul's voice shook when he said, "It weren't nothing like Father says."

Rebekah asked shyly, "Do flowers mean the earth is healing?"

Paul said, "Somewhat."

"Then give the flower to Father Ernst," she said. "Mayhap it's a sign for the Ascension. Time for our Deliverance." Rebekah lay her hand upon his chest. Was she checking his pulse?

Paul said, "I already showed Father. Only thing he done is give me a thrashing. Best get rid of it."

"I don't understand," said Ruth.

Rebekah said nothing but she squeezed Paul's fingers tight, tight.

Ruth twiddled the flower, imagined a garland of the purple blossoms to mount her dark hair for their union ceremony, dreamed of clasping Paul's hands, the signing of vows. But Rebekah took the flower and put it in her mouth. She chewed, chewed, swallowed. Smiled from sweetness. Then puckered from the last bitter traces.

Ruth lets go of the bars and sits on the cousin board. She reclines, blowing on her sore hands. Her heels stretch almost to the end. Seven years ago, the ham-radio news coverage of the Great Standoff wasn't what she had expected. Topside, nobody seemed to understand that God had commanded Father Ernst. That the Family was enacting God's will. Lists of the bombing victims' names were read aloud, for hours. Heart-wrenching stories, told and retold, by traumatized survivors. Down in the bunker, they sat and stewed until, filled with horror and remorse, some began to cry. Then Father Ernst shut off the radio and insisted they sing hymns instead.

Ruth's mind turns. She daren't think on the past, no matter what Paul says. The past is a dark bird, frantic, swooping, cawing at her. Ruth never knows how she'll feel when a memory appears, or if things will still add up as they are meant to in the Doctrine.

At hand now is her due Reflection, and Father Ernst will want to hear some wholesome pronouncements. Once Ruth clears her mind, it comes, plain as a picture—sin is like a wild dog that scrounges and spawns a dirty pack. One snarling beast in front—that's Ruth telling the wicked story. Trailing behind are all the other sins. Telling to impressionable girls, the vessels, more to the point. Then comes perjury; lying to Father Ernst. Begrudging Mother Susan, cursing the old woman's joyless vigil, that's also a sin. Casting blame on Rebekah, and on the nameless one who enchanted her with taboo tales in the first place, yet another whelp of sin!

Paul would have a different view if only he were here to untangle it like knotted string. He might say, 'How can telling a story be worse than stealing the Family's food?' Cousin Silas is often whipped but rarely locked away for his transgressions. Paul might ask, "Is eating ideas worse than eating the rotting oats?"

And then there'd be consequences.

Ruth felt Father Ernst tremble when he held her by the wrist and spoke of her womanhood, her impending bride time. How fierce he is, a wiry explosion of beard and moustache, the damning glint of his eyes filling her with dread. Femaleness is the problem: that much is clear. If Silas, if any boy had done what she did, would Father Ernst find it so depraved? She doubts it. Ruth's mind winds along villainous paths. She's in deeper, up to the hilt.

Footsteps approach and veer off elsewhere. The infirmary? Ruth strains to listen. Some quiet rummaging. More steps. Then comes the whisper of a sound to distract her—cotton skirts on the concrete floor—and Rebekah's solemn face peers in through the bars.

"Cousin," says Ruth. She presses herself to the gate.

Rebekah says nothing. Shadows fall from cheekbones, skeletal.

She is so changed in recent days. Musk comes in dank waves from her body, her dirty hair.

"Don't worry, I'll not say nothing about the book," says Ruth.

Not even a blink from Rebekah. Just the staring of those eyes, the pupils of which shine, dilated and wet.

Ruth whispers, "What's wrong?"

Rebekah won't answer.

An unnamed fear fills Ruth. "Tell me, please." She slides one stinging hand between the bars and flattens her palm. "If you cannot speak, do finger alphabet," she says. Before Rebekah became a mother, she and Ruth would lie awake for hours after the night bell talking just so, spelling out messages back and forth.

Rebekah presses a bony finger to Ruth's palm. It's like a candle stub, waxen and cold. Ruth winces. Rebekah seems to notice the whip welts. She flips Ruth's hand to use the backside instead, which is a blessing. But the backs of her hands are not as sensitive, and when Rebekah traces out the letters, Ruth is not sure. First is a capital 'G' or mayhap a 'Q'. Then a large 'U' and definitely the letter 'I' with its slash and dot and then an 'L'. She draws a letter 'T'—or is it the Holy cross?

A clattering erupts in the hall, and Mother Susan is upon them like a bent nail. She thrusts the wire broom and dustpan at Rebekah. "Must I carry the entire workload? Hie thee!" She flicks her apron to rush Rebekah away.

"And you, Cousin Ruth. This is punishment, not a tea party. You will break Father Ernst's heart yet with your wicked ways, don't I know the truth."

Ruth stutters, "I-I shan't."

"By the sign of your dark hair, I know you have invited the Devil inside."

"I have not," says Ruth. Why is Susan so mean?

"You're to sit the night," says Susan. "Not fit for the girls' company, not until Father Ernst has had his word with you."

Ruth sucks in her breath. Once, shortly after Hannah made her bride time, Ruth saw Father having a word with her, his door not quite shut. They were not words, they were actions—Father's hairy buttocks moving against Hannah's uplifted skirt, the sound of skin slapping skin, making her cry.

"Abide with me," says Ruth. Her voice hiccups. She reaches through the bars. "I cannot have a word, I'm not ready. Mother Susan, you know it's true."

"Mayhap you will be more judicious henceforth, Cousin. 'For in one hour so great riches is come to nought. For in one hour, is she made desolate.'"

When Susan turns, the soft ruffle of cotton hem on cement tears into Ruth. Susan's footsteps echo to quiet, all the way to nothing, and Ruth is more alone than she's ever been.

CHAPTER 10

Dear Sister. All of her letters begin the same way. Even in the quiet stillness of her own mind, Rebekah dares not use her Christian name, revoked during the casting-out. Rebekah composes with invisible ink, stores the letters in a mental corner, believes that if she concentrates hard enough she can send them like a radio frequency sends a song, with the power of her own conviction. This will have to do. For Rebekah hasn't a clue what township or city her sister might live in or if she is even still alive. And she can hardly get a real stamp or post an actual envelope. Do they still deliver the mail topside?

This was the first of so many:

Dear Sister,

Did you make it to New York City? I hope you coloured your hair auburn just as you wanted. I wonder if you wear pumps and stockings and lipstick. Imagine. I miss you. Bunker living is a boring stink hole of chores. You'd hate it.

All my love, Rebekah.

Today it is even more loathsome to wake and fairly impossible to swing her legs over the bedframe or shuffle into the blue dress. Susan barks, "Haul yourself." To her right is Ruth's empty bed—still locked in Contemplation. The little girls murmur things, Rebekah doesn't know what. A golden sunbeam beckons from cotton-candy clouds in that other dream world. She could curl in the fragrant grass and rest. She could lie on her back and watch the sky shift, minute to minute. Sing lullabies to the little wasted life inside. Then, small hands are patting her. Insistent. More shouting. She's not to lie abed taunting the Devil with slovenly thoughts with her wanton woman's body. She's to get up. She's to get to work! That Susan.

At long last, one thought rouses her: two pills left, taped and hidden. When the others are distracted she will fetch them. Keep them close, right in her pocket. There—at least she has some kind of plan. She begins a new letter.

Dear Sister,

Is this what it means to be in love? Hopeless in every hour, except for the one you spend with your beloved. Was it like this for you, so long ago? I have a hare-brained idea to find you, wherever you are. If I wait a little longer he promises to come too. Waiting—something I used to be quite good at—these many tainted years.

All my love, Rebekah

As a toddler, Rebekah fell down the rickety basement stairs in Mother Deborah's house, arse over teakettle, and lay on the cement floor undiscovered for hours. Father Ernst was away on a speaking tour, and the boys were out in the field. Deborah was putting up the pickles and beets, had lugged jars and the oversized canner from downstairs, forgetting to latch the door. She sterilized lids in the steamy kitchen and kept the oven at a solid temperature to heat the Mason jars, which she lined up on baking sheets like soldiers. She iced cucumbers in the large sink—her secret extra step—to give them more crunch. It was hard work, and Mother Mary was to have helped but had stayed in bed with the flu. Deborah trimmed the vegetables with her favourite paring knife, the sharpest, the one with the plastic handle. Beet juice stained her fingers bright pink and dripped down the front of her pale apron. She stirred in sugar, salt, spices, and set the brine pots to simmer. She paused, mopping sweat from her brow. An unknown urgency overcame her, and she circled the ground and upper floors, even the little-used attic room, but could not locate her youngest child. Outside, calling her name around the garden and to the edge of the field. She ran back to the house, inside, and noticed the basement door ajar.

All of this Rebekah knows because she floated there, slightly above and behind her mother's carefully parted and combed hair, while her twisted little body lay unmoving at the foot of the stairs.

The county doctor was summoned, and he diagnosed her with head trauma, concussion. It was serious, he said. Deborah followed his orders precisely, setting up the attic room for her convalescence, stripping it of colour, and covering the windows with thick curtains. Weeks passed. No music, no games. Not even the dogs allowed to visit. Rebekah sipped tepid broth and warm, watery oats. Deborah usually brought the meals and sat on the edge of the narrow bed to spoon-feed her, distraught, guilt colouring her cheeks.

When Father Ernst returned, sated from tour, he researched experimental treatments, and so Rebekah's head was iced at regular intervals and she was made to wear a blindfold during daylight hours. He almost never visited the cramped upper room. Something about the way she lay so still unnerved him. Rebekah's sense of smell became acute. She sometimes vomited from nausea when wafts of frying bacon reached her from the main floor kitchen, and she begged them to cease. Lying in bed blindfolded, her hearing, her hands, especially the tips of her fingers, became sharply perceptive. She had to remain calm, prone, regardless of newly violent impulses that wracked her small body. Regardless of the bold and frightening pictures, the visions invading her sleep, taking hold of her imagination. She spent days, weeks, in this Otherworld, pulled back to attic room realness only when someone arrived with medication or a cup of tea or a bowl of wholesome soup.

Her teenage sister, whom she adored, would break Father Ernst's rule and sneak upstairs. Sometimes she scaled the house siding and propped a ladder on the porch roof in order to climb through an attic window. "Aren't you lonely?" she'd say and tear off Rebekah's blindfold. "How else will you see the drawings?" She read from a forbidden book—fairy tales—one she had discovered at a rummage sale and secreted home in her skirts. Her sister pulled out the nails from a loose floorboard in the attic room and tucked the book inside. "Now you can look whenever you like," she said.

"I'm not to get out of bed," said Rebekah. "Only for the chamber pot."

"Nonsense," said her sister. "You'll waste away. You need to get strong again. Even Rapunzel escapes."

"Read me that one again," said Rebekah, shifting against the stacked pillows.

"Read it yourself."

"The letters go blurry."

"Fine. But follow along with my finger."

Rebekah had little choice but to retreat into that great pool of fantasy in the book and also in her mind. Over the years it served her well. She was a happy, if somewhat aloof, child. She told no one but her sister about the secret world. They agreed: surely it was God's Garden, the glorious place Father Ernst spoke of in sermons and in their nightly prayers. He'd be livid to know she could come and go on her own, without following his many Doctrine rules, wouldn't he?

By the next summer, Rebekah was back in the shared bedroom, doing light chores alongside everyone else. The Family would jokingly refer to that worrisome period as Rebekah's Fall from Grace. Young Thomas would, without warning, stiffen like a board and teeter slowly to the ground shouting, "Who am I?" setting off gales of laughter. They could have fun sometimes, before.

At Father Ernst's insistence, her sister landed part-time secretarial work at the local medical clinic. "I get to use computers," she said, beaming. On the Farm, none of the females were allowed. Then one night while they lay in bed, she whispered, "I'm to get a hold of the X-ray equipment supplies." Rebekah could not fathom why. "They want it. To make bombs," she said. Her hand, when it gripped Rebekah's, was very cold.

Things changed after that. Her sister became furtive and withdrawn. She was home less often. Rebekah heard her sneaking out the bedroom window at night and creeping back in at dawn, her body reckless with adventure, skin lit by a clandestine flame. There was a boy, somewhere. Rebekah covered for her time and again, but eventually she was caught. Then, the casting-out. How could a boy, how could anything be terrible enough to warrant that? A solemn lesson learned, for shame.

How they wept.

Now Rebekah is about the age that her sister was then, eighteen, and the pattern repeats. Despite the terrifying impression the ritual left on her childhood self, Rebekah, in the here and now, recreates her sister's dilemma. Rebekah skulks and lies. She breaks commandments and revels in sin as much as her sister ever did. Leads a young man into temptation. Into danger. Loses herself in desire. In her quiet desperation, Rebekah snares Paul, who is trusting and kind and doesn't yet know about the fragile life growing inside her. She has no right and every right to tell him. Had he known, would he still have left her below?

What kind of monster is she?

Human, she longs to shout. For isn't it a simple question of nature? The unrepentant song of the flesh, joyous and sacred. Bodies coiled together in heat, minds and spirits united in love. Why is this seditious?

But she knows it is dangerous. It threatens the fabric, the structure, and the future of their small colony. One will eat the other, surely. What is duty? Rebekah would happily abandon everything—the bunker, the children, the Doctrine, and all of Father Ernst's many rules—for a chance to experience real pleasure away from this shadow of shame. And if *she* would break the bond of her covenant, so too would others. The great unravelling. There'd be no Family, no Farm, after all. It only works when they all play their part, especially the mothers. Paul believes he can tend the wildness of their private calling and still keep his obligations to the Family, the children. But it's impossible—he cannot protect them all. And she, seemingly, cannot protect anyone, not even herself.

He, noble boy, will eventually succumb to Family pressures. Yet she will choose Paul over the rest of them, again and again, if she has the chance. This will be the crux of their downfall.

"Who am I?" she says, lying on her lonely cot.

Little girls crowd around. "Mother Rebekah," says one, "are you okay?" Whispering, cooing, like pigeons.

In Rebekah's vivid memory, young brother Thomas sprawls on the wide, sanded boards of the front porch imitating her, and the Family gathers round, guffawing. He was such a funny kid. Rebekah begins to laugh—an abrupt hacking sound—startling the girl at her elbow and alarming the twins who hover nearby.

Rebekah says, "Who am I?"

The children back away.

"Should we get Mother Susan?" asks one.

"No, she'll shout at us all."

More whispers.

Reflecting back on her Fall from Grace, Rebekah is certain that period of her early life—the nearly fatal accident and its long, slow recovery—single-handedly prepared her for the then-unimaginable future as Father Ernst's fifth wife.

Dear Sister,

The truth is sharp-toothed and ravenous. Love or no love, if I could survive on my own I'd have left already. I can cook but not hunt. Harvest but not plant. What I'm good for is to service a family, a man. I cannot defend myself here or topside. I can keep house but not build one. What a terrible, terrible oversight. Don't you agree?

All my love, Rebekah

CHAPTER 11

Paul follows sage scent and sits at the base of the shrub to rest the Ruger beside him, legs stretched in front. He removes the gas mask to wipe his face. He can go without it now; the air smells fresh, and mosquitoes buzz in multitude. He lowers the zipper on his coveralls, slips his arms out. Unscrews the top of his canteen and drinks deeply. Water on lips and tongue, swishing in his mouth, water down the throat. Swallowing, swallowing and belching, deep like a pond frog. He licks his salty lips and drinks again, long and slow.

A clear night with lots of visible stars. Sand shimmers in the light of the gibbous moon. Like satin or silk, like the women's lingerie he peeked at in Memaw's mail-order catalogues. Fingertip-slick paper, dog-eared—brassieres and gartered stockings and corsets—that he secreted to the outhouse where he ogled squares and rectangles of women, parts of the whole. Taboo pleasure. Guilt souring it, after.

He unlaces the boots and kicks them off, dumps out sand that has collected, pulls his legs from the coveralls. Holds his feet in his hands, one at a time. Blisters have come up where the boots rub. A breeze cools his swollen feet, his aching body. It is hard to tell exactly how far he's come, but he thinks he's made good time. Still an hour before dawn. The hardest time to stay awake but most pivotal. He has encountered nothing so far, no predators or travellers. No rebel campfires in the distance. So much for the fabled resistance. He'll need shelter if he wants to sleep and food to keep up his strength.

The Family would be sleeping now. Silas and Abel in their shared room, snoring, groaning like spectres in the night. Springs squeaking discreetly. Bunks, end to end, twin mattresses, storage trunks below. A map of the Farm on one wall, ominous portrait of Father Ernst above it. Those painted eyes follow the boys, penetrating the dark. Paul sees it as though he is still bunkered, lying awake on his cot. Fusty scent of unwashed boys: sweat and traces of urine. Stagnant air. Wafts of the latrine, next door. Listening for tell-tale creaks. The door. Rebekah, come to him again in the night. Leading him to the dark pantry, the empty hall, or down the cold tunnel.

The beds were meant to be full of children and toddlers. Instead, they each get a double bunk to themselves, plus extras. Their tribe is not flourishing, contrary to what Father Ernst preaches from the Doctrine. Despite his many wives, his endless opportunities to breed, their numbers dwindle. Now more than ever the boys pose a threat, and Father's ambivalence is palpable. He bullies Silas, whom he neutered and whose job is to preserve the Doctrine. And Paul himself Father Ernst has always loathed. Paul knows this in his bones. If Father Ernst ever discovered him with Rebekah, he'd kill them both, starting with her. He'd make Paul suffer by watching.

Paul clenches his fists. Topside, things are clear. It's not easy living, but there is possibility. Rebekah has wanted to escape ever since she'd been made a wife. "Please," she whispered. "Let's go." She begged to join him during his last forage, to disappear together, forever. In the end, he could not go through with it, couldn't leave his sister behind, and Ruth still needs convincing.

Paul can feel his dad's hands gripping his ten-year-old boy arms, bruising them, the day they went to ground. "I leave Ruth in your care. You're all she's got. Promise me."

Ruth and he believed their dad would be bunkering with them, but Father Ernst had other plans. Men surrounded and held him. He shouted for Paul to descend with the mothers and the children. Paul screamed and fought until he was hoisted over a broad shoulder and hauled away. He remembers struggling, crying, watching his dad get smaller as men—members of their congregation—dragged him in the opposite direction, chained him to the front door of the church, fitted him with the padded Martyr vest lined with explosives, Family emblem stitched front and back.

Forced to Martyr. Later, stripped of his name, shamed as a traitor anyway.

So Paul is sworn to protect Ruth, biding time. But the longer they wait, the weaker they become. Could he even carry her up the ladder, the way he himself was forced down it as a boy? Not likely. One last time he will bring food for the Family. Then they must leave. Time is running out.

Pitter-patter. A slithering—the detectable sound of movement alerts Paul. The Ruger is up, safety clicked off, wide eyes aiming through the night-vision scope. He steps away from his gear, pours his body forward, bare feet in the dirt, squatting to kneel, silent. Movement in the scrub grass several yards away, a furred thing up in the air, down. Jackrabbit, with those tall ears. Paul hesitates, then sets the Ruger down carefully. A gunshot would carry over the sands, alerting anyone to his whereabouts. He reaches for the stick instead. The hare leaps, bounds. Paul aims for the space ahead of it, waits. Leaves his body, rides the breeze closer, hovers. That other self, the shadow hunter, hurls the stick. Strikes the target. Paul jogs to the brush, knife ready. The hare hiccups and twitches, spent.

He should be proud, but what Paul feels is closer to shame. Perhaps it had a mate and offspring who now must make their way in the world alone. Must he always kill to survive? He says, "Father in Heaven, your bounty sustains us. Amen."

He gathers dried grasses, dead branches, husks from desiccated plants for a fire and sweeps a hollow in the sand. Sets the grass fluff in the centre, props the bigger pieces above like a tepee. In his deep pocket is a tiny Mason jar of strike-anywhere matches, and he lights one against the lid, which is covered in sandpaper. He cups his hands. It catches on the dried tinder. Orange burst, golden light dancing on fingers. Flame eats the kindling, and he slips larger sticks over top. Fire will keep most predators away—wild dogs run miles for a fresh rabbit—but might attract humans. He keeps the Ruger and his stick within reach while he cleans and preps the hare. He slits the belly, squeezes shut and carefully cuts the bladder out, the intestines, the organs, the spine. He'll leave this pile for a coyote, an offering. Cuts strips of flesh, skewers them on sharp sticks, and sets them up around the fire. While they cook, he works on the hare's pelt. He will not waste anything; dried and stretched, this fur will keep one of the children warm. Rebekah could fashion it into something useful.

The spit sizzle of juice dripping on coals makes him ravenous. Paul waits as long as he can before tearing off a piece and filling his mouth. It's not smart to eat meat when he's dehydrated—breaking down dense food uses up even more of the body's moisture. But the rich, wet chew, a watering in his mouth, awakens him. He'll have one piece now and wrap the rest in yucca leaves for the Family.

Could he lure them out with this meat? Through the tunnel, up the ladder, out the heavy blast doors to the hot sands. The way he used to lead horses in weather—their ears flattened to thunder, nostrils flared, huge beasts jittery with fright. A handful of oats from the pail, a carrot or apple to urge them forward. The shuck-stamp of hooves in the field, bump and sway of gleaming haunches, giant eyes rolling, gateway to a soul unknown. He had to get the horses before panic took root. That veneer of training—acquired habits and familiar routines, the order humans force upon them—falls away in the true face of terror. Once, Paul saw them stampede. The massive stallion and a glossy black mare churning pasture mud, racing against lightning, screaming into the storm. Part of him thrilled when they leapt the fence, never looking back. Still, he wept, knowing how likely they were to be carried in flash floods along the creek bed, or caught up in barbed-wire fencing that tracked most of the county. Painful deaths awaited—broken legs and slow drowning. The stallion survived, was never quite the same. The mare did not.

Was it worth the run, that brief eruption of chaos? At the time, Paul thought no. Now, he is not sure.

Provider. His contract is to serve the Family, absolutely. One role or nothing—Father Ernst has made that clear. In their stale cramped quarters it makes sense. There's no room for confusion, for any challenge to his leadership. But here, topside, he is alone and not alone. Here he can live by wits and instinct and skill. His dad might as well be sitting across the fire from him now. His dad lives in the Ruger, in the sparking flames, and in those unremitting wild stirrings, deep inside.

CHAPTER 12

The broom and pan are propped in the kitchen alcove, but it's obvious the floors have not been swept. There was a time when the mothers sang as they worked together—Memaw, Deborah, and Mary. Gone to God's Garden, all three, taking joy with them. Susan has already wiped the table and benches, already hoisted them on top of the table to prepare the floors. On top of that, she cleaned the kitchen.

"I'm to do everything, am I? I'm the mule!"

Susan yanks the broomstick and begins to whisk it, raising dust that coats her lips and teeth, her dry tongue, choking her. She coughs. Her eyes water and she can't see. She throws the broom down and hacks, hacks, spits. Fury consumes her, and she surprises herself with a brief but violent cry. She wipes her face with her dress sleeve and takes a deep breath.

The creaking wheels of the stationary bike startle her. It's Silas, that goose. She didn't notice him.

"Get to bed," she says, and he slides off the seat.

"Are, are you all right?" he says.

"Get."

The boy's shoulders hunch with worry but he goes.

She straightens herself. Nonsense. This is Rebekah's chore, and she shall do it. Laying abed, not a peep out of her and not one stick of work done—that's not the Family way. Girls today are spoiled, that's what. They don't know how good they have it.

In the women's quarters, the little girls flock around Rebekah's cot. The twins scatter when Susan strides into the room, but Leah remains close, whispering. Rebekah lies very still.

"Rise, Mother Rebekah," says Susan. "You got chores, so haul yourself."

No answer from the bed.

"Mayhap you despise it, but I'll not do it alone," says Susan. "Dreaming is the Devil's work, and you shall not service him under my nose."

Susan grabs Rebekah's cup and flings the last bit of water in her face. The girls jump. Rebekah remains silent, unblinking. Droplets run over her pale brow, pool in the concave ponds that house her staring eyes. Drops stand on her cheeks, her dry lips, and spackle the neck of her nightgown.

Leah burrows like a small animal, licking coveted drops from Rebekah's face. "Get down," says Susan, but Leah will not. "In your own bed, now." Susan swats her rear end, and Leah scuttles out of reach.

"You got the rage come on?" says Susan. She shakes the small lump at the bottom of the bed—Rebekah's foot.

Nothing.

She jams the loose sheet ends under the mattress, in case Rebekah begins to roll in Godly possession. Susan turns a grim face upon the little girls. "Pray for her."

The twins clasp hands under their chins. Leah kneels on her own cot. They say the Fits prayer together. "God, watch over Mother

Rebekah. Keep her safe from demons, guide her visions, and bring goodly tidings of our vindication, our glorious Ascension. Amen."

"Now get in there," Susan says, and snaps off the light. "There'll be no stories tonight." She unties her apron at the waist, lifts it over her head, and hangs it on the nail beside her cot. She reaches over her shoulder for the dress zipper and pulls it down an inch or two. She stretches up behind her back but cannot grasp the zipper. She tries and tries. She hates to ask for help, but her back is paining. Fiery streaks ramp up without relief.

"Helen," she hisses. "Get my dress, will you?"

The child slips from her bed and creeps over, wide-eyed. She pulls the zipper down, over the dreaded hump, all the way past the waist into the flared skirt. "There," she whispers.

"That'll do, " says Susan.

Susan shimmies to lift the dress over her head. That goes to the nail as well. Then the thick stockings, the worn slip. She stoops for a nightshirt and tumbles it over her head, pulls it down into place.

"Goodnight, Mother," says Helen.

The girl startles her, still at Susan's elbow. She vanishes and Susan hears the small cot squeak as she settles in again. Susan grips the cotton gown tightly in her fist. *Mother*.

What a peculiar sensation inhabits her just now. Susan sits on her own cot and lifts her heavy legs. She slowly reclines. She must turn to one side; the nerves pinch and stab at her. There was an ointment made from turmeric and comfrey root that Memaw used to mercifully rub in after a hard day, also long gone.

Night creeps through the chamber, and soon the girls are sleeping. Their snorts and tiny nose whistles sing a midnight song. Rebekah hasn't stirred once. Susan is bone-tired yet cannot sleep. Time wends, and eyes open or eyes closed, Susan's mind trips and stutters. It's all up to her. Father Ernst has nothing to do with the actual procuring of sustenance. He only speaks of it in grand terms. The oats. How many watery bowls can she wring from them yet? Never thought she'd starve, coming to live on a farm.

Cousin Paul will, God willing, return with roots. Greens. Something. But when? Water is low, and Father Ernst won't answer her on that. The topside drought has taken its toll on the water table in recent months and the well is run dry. They've got a half tank left. If only they'd stored more when they had the chance.

Coughs rattle someone's small lungs—Rachel, she thinks. The child shifts and spits without waking, so familiar is this affliction. Susan rolls to her back and over to her other side, and the cot squeaks her distress with each shift and turn. She sighs. Night is the dark angel's realm, when sin strikes fierce.

Ruth is locked in Contemplation, and Hannah is still in Father Ernst's chamber, been there hours. She is sometimes permitted to sleep in that large feather bed. Plenty enough room in his chamber, Susan knows. She has to clean it. If only Father Ernst would be more discreet with some of his belongings. Things she can never unsee. The magazine, for one. Men can't help it. Still, he is a Christian leader. It's terrible to think of him flipping those pages and stroking himself or the girl, allowing such barbaric images to curdle his lust.

Susan took time to look through it herself, pulled by horror and by some other twisting need that confused and shamed her thoroughly. The women in the magazine looked like none she's seen on God's earth. Breasts larger than their heads, surgical scars sometimes gaping from underneath the swells. Tiny waists, flat behinds, and no body hair anywhere other than the obscene strips between their dolly legs, like old time vertical moustaches, confounding her. The two women together—that was an electric horror. Susan thinks of them still: tongues touching as they spread their hindquarters for the camera. Skinny legs and knobby knees, like foals.

Susan presses her thighs together and heat builds. Under the silent blanket she moves, furtive. She pinches her nipples. Bites her lip. Takes hot, shallow breaths. Slow circles, she imagines a tongue reaching, a small lapping at private skin folds. She squeezes and releases her muscles below the waist and tries not to creak the bed. An agony builds and her thighs grow slick. Susan gasps and breathes out her shaky mouth, cools herself, does it again. And again. Brings herself to the brink of destruction and holds to that nauseous tip. Her straining body shakes the bedframe.

Lightning flares in her back, pain rips her rounded shoulders. He strikes where sin festers—a punishment of eternal fire. Susan releases the held breath. The arch of her left foot cramps, and she cannot reach it, she cannot hold it in her hands and massage the knot away and there is no one to do it for her. She gnashes her teeth in pain. She could weep a black sorrow. *God forgive my shame.*

The heels of her hands press against her eye sockets. She mouths a silent prayer. Steadies her nerves and tries to flex her left toes and then point them, but the knot spasms. She stifles a cry. After God, it is the ghost of Memaw Ruth she beseeches. Memaw's merciful hands, the kindest she's ever known. What she'd give for a haunting.

CHAPTER 13

Ruth scrapes, scrapes the blade of her knife, whetstone in swollen hand. The movement, the sound, of sharpening soothes her nerves. The cousin board is hard and splintery. It is very cold in the chamber, cold and damp. She has no blanket, just her regular shirt, trousers, and a thinning sweater. The thick belt, woollen socks, worn slippers. She stands and paces for circulation. She sits to rest. A meanness brews in her belly and lower, in some invisible, tormented female part. Her bladder presses but Ruth resists, not wanting to drop her drawers in the chill.

Hours pass in the dark cell, and Susan does not come. Nor Cousin Silas to mock her with scripture readings and then to moon and blush wordlessly. Nor the children, little ratstickers. They must be in bed. Ruth slides her knife back into its sheath at her belt. She needs water and another morsel of food. She misses her cot—a night of exile and she will gladly overlook its creaking shortfalls: lumpy mattress, flat pillow.

After a time, she cannot lie on the cousin board for cold, and she cannot pace the cell for weakness. Her lower back thrums, and an unfamiliar beast claws at her loins. Cold or not, Ruth undoes her belt, unbuttons her trousers with numb fingers. She squats over the bucket but nothing comes, only a burning that makes her cry. Finally, the hot stream. When she bends to look, the dull light reveals Ruth's smeared thighs and underwear pooling black. Ripe with metallic heat, like a dying thing. Poison! Rotting her insides?

What unholy trespass, this?

Ruth steadies her breath, and Hannah's description of the moon time taunts: "You bloat and weep and ache beyond the woman hole, and nasty drips splooge into your pants."

Alas, this deluge likely signals Ruth's inevitable womanly anguish, not death by disease. She daren't ask Hannah—the only thread keeping their kinship is Ruth's child status. And Susan is impossible. Only Rebekah, humane and meek, might reveal this terrible mystery.

Ruth balls up the ruined undergarment and wipes herself as best she can. Blood has seeped through her trousers, staining them. The floor is mottled with it. Now her fingers are red-tipped. Everything she touches, she taints. Just like her future, which unfolds before her: bride rites, birthing, mothering. Hard-worked, just to be charred for the eventual sacred pouch. Ruth folds the bloody garment and lines the crotch of her trousers with it to sop up the mess. She re-buttons the fly, closes her belt. She wipes her hands on the leg of her pants. Is there a worse fate? She'd rather martyr herself topside, armed to the teeth, hurling grenades of glory at the wicked. She'd fight them one by one, raving from the Doctrine until they whimpered and confessed their heinous burdens: baby killers, homosexuals, communists. Melt them with Godly convictions; make the Family proud.

Anything is better than taking up the motherdress.

Once, when she glorified the Martyrs, Paul said, "Shut up, Ruth. They weren't brave. They were locked out of the bunker."

"Blasphemer."

"It's the truth," he hissed. "You won't hear it from no one else."

"Martyrs make the noble brethren sacrifice."

"Not one left to disagree," he said. Paul's voice was choked with feeling.

Paul. Waging his own war, he's got more to worry about than Ruth's woman body betraying her at last. Him, digging tubers from earth littered with mines. Shaking the branches of mutilated fruit trees, bomb survivors from the old orchard. Trailing tracks, dowsering water. Picking mushrooms, wild greens, and healing mosses from the shrinking forest, hiking desert sands. All whilst hiding from government spies and wandering maniac tribes, heretics who propagate the unclean masses.

Ruth could cry. She has one hope: Paul returns bearing signs and portents for their imminent Ascension before anyone learns her female pronouncement—this dread body truth. If Father Ernst can be convinced to leave the bunker, mayhap she will not have to marry him. Then she and Paul could be united topside, as in her dreams. They could rebuild the old cabin. She could keep him clean and cared for. Give herself to that. She wouldn't mind.

A jangling at the gate: keys in Father Ernst's hands, his heavy tang hovering like an unkind fog. "How is your sleep, Cousin?"

Ruth sits on her hands to hide their stain. "Fine, Father." She blushes. "I mean I didn't at all, to state the truth strictly."

A small movement about his mouth—is it a smile? Ruth can't tell because the moustache and beard obscure.

"Have you given over to Contemplations, Cousin?"

"Yes, Father. I summed up my many faults. I made a list."

Father Ernst's calloused hand turns the key in the gate lock. "A list is not necessary. It's more important to understand what is required of a woman. That is what I wish to speak about." He opens the gate and enters.

Ruth's throat heats. Tickle becomes rumble and she coughs.

Father Ernst sits close beside her on the bench. Can he smell the blood on her? Ruth's coughing persists, and she covers her mouth with a sleeve. She leans away from him. His large hand rests on the back of her neck. He rubs the muscles, the tendons. He strokes her back and that does not help the coughing, but he does not stop either. His other hand warms her thigh. Through her watering eyes she sees grey tufts sprouted from his knuckles. Blood spotted faintly on the fabric beside it. *God in Heaven.*

Ruth prays for cousin shadows, for rustling skirts, for any intrusion at all.

"Do you know what you need, Cousin?"

Ruth croaks, "Water. A sip." She pulls her hands up inside her long sleeves to hide her fingers. She crosses her sleeved arms in front.

Father Ernst says, "Not yet. First we need to talk about the Family, our Holy tribe. As you know, our pledge is to defend God in these uncertain times. We are his earth army. And each soldier has a role. Yours will be to bear children and to raise them, strong and pure, in my service to God's Holy name. Maintaining my pure lineage: this is the single most important job. Without children, there is no future. Without a future, we are nothing and God is lost, forever."

"Father," she whispers, "I would offer the most noble brethren sacrifice, Martyr for the Family. For you and for God. Please."

Father Ernst pulls her closer and keeps his arm around her. He pets her hair, ruffles it, and leans his prickly beard against her. "My girl," he says, "let me tell you something. We must choose to do as God says, not as we like. Otherwise we do not serve anyone but ourselves."

Ruth sighs.

"Soon you will be a woman. Very soon."

Now is the time to tell him. Ruth opens her mouth. She closes it.

Father Ernst pulls a Martyr card from his robe pocket and holds it where she can see. It's Ruth, companion to the weary, she who saved others from evil. Memaw Ruth's portrait is edged with flowers, ropey vines, and two bluebirds sing above her head. The card is faded from handling. Everyone's favourite.

"My first wife, gentle and wise. She was lovely. Like our only child, our daughter, also named Ruth. Your birth mother."

Ruth says nothing. Her limbs grow stiff. Here comes the past, shrieking.

"You never knew her, of course, but you have her eyes. Their eyes. Their mannerisms. Reminds me of a golden time."

Ruth counts silently to stay calm. *One, one thousand, two, one thousand, three ...*

"That is why I have great faith in you. You shall bear me many babes. Our tribe will swell in numbers and only then shall we rise, unstoppable in God's name."

"But—the Ascension—"

"Will wait for our progeny. Your children. I have seen this in a dream."

"It can't be." Ruth cannot get enough air into her lungs.

"It can be. It must. I have seen you lead the children up the ladder. I have seen you carry them, swaddled, at your breast."

A chasm tears open Ruth's chest. Sharp pains squeeze, squeeze her heart, crushing it.

"Memaw understood her role. Queen of the mothers. Morally impeccable, loving, kind. Some see it as weakness, but that is hateful liberal thinking. That is a lie. Woman's natural strength is her innate goodness. When woman conquers temptation, she is beyond reproach. She is an angel walking the earth. *This* is what God wants, what you must accept. Not firing guns or giving sermons to heathens. That is men's work, Ruth. And you must leave these childish whims behind, once and for all, your trousers, rat traps, this play at hunting. It is unbecoming of my future bride, of a cousin mother."

Ruth's whole body thrums with a panic she cannot name. She thinks of Hannah, who shimmies with pride to be offered as a Holy Vessel unto Father Ernst. Not Ruth. If Father Ernst sees the blood trace on her clothes or in the bucket, he'd take her in a heartbeat. Here in the cold cell, on the filthy cement.

"Do you understand?"

Ruth nods although she does not know what he is saying, exactly.

"Do you have any questions about the bridal rite?" Father Ernst squeezes her thigh.

Ruth stares. Why must she do it at all?

"You may ask anything. About that or about motherhood."

"Well. Couldn't I do things I'm good at, in God's service? I'm hopeless in the kitchen."

"You have been given a child's leeway, allowed to do as you like. You have not put your mind to learning these more important tasks," he says. Father Ernst removes the ties from her hair as he talks. He tugs the braids loose, freeing sections of Ruth's oily locks. "You will become good at them. That is your job. We've no room for those who don't earn their keep."

Ruth steadies herself on the pallet.

"Mother Susan and I will be watching you closely. Is that understood?"

Ruth nods.

"I've brought you something to quicken your blood tide."

Now again would be the right time to share this truth: that it has already come upon her like a thief.

He procures a small white cube from his pocket and holds it between thumb and first finger. *Sugar.*

The Family ran out of sugar during the fourth winter below after a long rationing that meant fewer pies and loaves, and no surplus grains to balance the bitter swallow of roasted chicory root tea.

"How do you still have sugar?" She is lost in a reverie of beloved lemon pastries, raisin bread, jams, and current tarts. She remembers tiny doughnuts that Memaw fried and sprinkled with cinnamon.

Father Ernst says, "This is kept in my Vestal cabinet, along with all my sacred tools. All my precious treats. As a wife, a mother, you will sometimes share them."

Ruth reaches but he shakes his head. He fluffs her dark hair around her shoulders. "You look like her. Darker, but still ..."

Father Ernst places it on Ruth's tongue. Hard, sharp-cornered, it takes a moment for her mouth to respond. Saliva pools and begins to soften the cube. Then comes sweetness, a wet mouthful. Ruth sucks and the cube clatters against her molars. She nibbles; more hits of the sugary rush. Teeth jangle, blood livens, a siren wails inside her. Father Ernst leans close. His fingers wind loose strands of her hair. His wiry beard scratches her chin and neck, dances on her collarbones. Ruth leans back against the damp wall. Her lungs hold to bursting and then she has no choice; she must inhale his rank breath. Her hand floats to the knife at her belt. His body presses closer. His hands, strong on her arms, push them to the wall, trapping her. Then the stifling kiss: her first. It quashes everything nesting inside.

"Husband." The voice is shrill. Hannah skulks at the gate, arms crossed.

Father Ernst strokes Ruth's face. His calloused finger presses her lips. "Mother Susan shall come for you anon." He hoists himself from the bench, shuts the gate behind him. He grabs a surprised Hannah and pulls her close.

Hannah's face is white fury. Ruth is glad for the strong gate, the metal bars, between them.

Father Ernst says, "The bridal role is vital. Mothers extoll grace, patience, and chastity. Envy is one of the seven deadly sins, Cousin Hannah, and you shall no longer indulge it."

"But I'm the bride, not Ruth," she says.

"You are my sixth, and soon I shall take my seventh," says Father. "God has spoken. You must settle this now, Cousin Hannah. We are one Holy tribe. You are one mother, together."

Ruth's sugar cube clinks against her teeth. Her tongue dabs cracked lips, wetting them.

Hannah lunges, shrieking an animal sound, but Father holds her tight. He pushes her to kneeling, frowns. He looks tired, grey-faced. "God have mercy upon you," he says. He reopens the gate with one hand and waves Ruth out. When he shoves Hannah inside, the girls bump shoulders, hard.

Ruth cradles the spot where the bruise will come up. The gate locks behind her, and though she should feel glad of an early release, the foaming hiss from Hannah's curled lip worries her. She ducks her head when Father Ernst speaks.

"Until the rage shall pass and the Holy spirit amass, await His Contemplations, Amen."

CHAPTER 14

Morning bowls hold grey water, two spoons each. The soft fast. Tomorrow, the hard fast. Father Ernst scans the table: dismal, drawn faces. Silence. Mother Susan hunches at the kitchen alcove, swinging the empty ladle. She claims Mother Rebekah will not get up. Hannah stews in the Chamber of Contemplation. Ruth sits on the bench, trembling and coy. She's hiding something. What?

Women are not as they used to be. They slip through his fingers, confounding him. Turning away from God's Doctrine to some introspective puzzle he cannot fathom. It's eating them from the inside. They used to sit transfixed for hours while he spun story and sermon and Bible verse. They laughed and gasped and clutched at one another as soup simmered on the stovetop, bread baked in the oven. Cousin mothers were always at the heart of his joy, nursing infants while toddlers careened about. Rounded wombs: promises guarded by apron shields. The mothers loved him. Their scheduled visits to his chamber were electric.

Father Ernst clears his throat. His fingers comb wild hair. Once it was neat and cut short. Memaw regularly trimmed his beard. He feels for wiry ends that stretch along his flowing robe. Over the years he has changed too. But not his convictions. Not about the Doctrine and not about the Family's purpose.

Many pairs of watery blue eyes behold him now. One rebel set blinks darkly.

He begins. "The low-calorie diet is a blessing, and fasting is vital to the Doctrine."

"Praise be," they say. The children clasp hands to pray.

He says, "So shall we soft fast the sixth day. Let us prepare our bodies for God. Swallow His water and prepare for His gifts on the morrow. Then shall we hard fast the seventh. Neither water nor grain nor any sustenance shall pass our lips, for that day we give ourselves over to Him. That day we sit mindfully, lest He share a morsel of spiritual nourishment in the form of Holy visions."

"Amen, amen."

Father Ernst nods. Small hands grasp spoons, spoons rise to mouths, eyes shut to swallow. He counts blond heads along the bench. He loses track and starts over. Never mind the precise number, the main thing is there are so many empty spots. His tribe is shrinking

One: Silas, son of Mary, with thinning hair and turned-up nose, full lips, and the ghost of a double chin. He was plump once. Like he had a winter coat of his own flesh, and during the last years it had been unbuttoned, rolled up, put to storage someplace else. Silas had been gelded and set to task studying and preserving the Doctrine. He was useless in every other capacity, and besides, someone needed to take notes. He is no replacement for Jeremiah, groomed as Ernst's Second. Still, he kept track of Ernst's Holy revelations. He tried to please. Now the visions come so infrequently, the boy is basically redundant.

Two: Paul. Despite being topside on mission, the dark one still mocks him from his empty place on the bench, as though his brooding essence remains trapped below with the Family. Silas's opposite, Paul is argumentative. Rebellious. Yet he is an able hunter with strong foraging skills and so was spared his manhood, the two things being intrinsically connected.

Three. Father Ernst's eyes flit to the ventilation shaft above, follow the wavering line of a crack in the cement all the way over to the corner. Dark tendrils of movement. What watches him from the shadows? Who goes there?

A small sound to his left draws him back to table. He had been counting. Counting what?

Silas catches Father Ernst's eye and flashes a furtive smile, spoon held mid-air. Father nods. "Stand tall, Cousin."

The boy pales. He looks about the table, fearful, but gets to his feet. He says, "Reflections?"

"No, Cousin." Father Ernst strides close and runs a hand along his shoulders, down his back, tapping limbs like Silas is a beast of burden. "You are coming on to manhood," he says, and Silas beams. "You are strong enough to patch pipes and reinforce the cistern, I think."

Silas says, "Yes, Father. With your blessing."

"Wonderful," says Father Ernst. Let him pump the generator a few more days. Get the heavy work done while he can.

Ernst squints: steak flanks, fatty back rib strips, ham hock thighs and calves. Cousin Martyr, what the prophet Jesus gave unto his people, feeding them from his flesh, slaking thirst with his own blood: the ultimate, most noble sacrifice.

"Sit," he says, and the boy resumes drinking.

Father Ernst is tired but he must lead. Still standing above Silas, he booms, "In the beginning!"

"In the beginning," they say.

"In the beginning there was darkness, and there was the light."

Their mouths open for song:

"Yea, darkness fell upon the land
Yea, darkness fell upon His hand
The Devil flew in blackened skies
The people, they succumbed to Lies
Lust and Greed and Gluttony
Sloth, Wrath, Pride, Envy
Idolatry and Fornication
Brought demise to our great nation
Smite the wicked, set them bound,
And burn the heathens to the ground!
Burn the heathens to the ground!"

Father Ernst conducts the boys' bench to begin again, this time singing in rounds. He sings with Silas and little Abel. He motions the girls to join in after the first verse. Their thin voices bring warmth to the room, and although it's not the glory of the former Family gatherings, it is something. He walks back to the head of the table and sits, waves his hand in time until the last notes sound. He locks eyes with Ruth and her hands grip the table edge. "Burn the heathens to the ground!"

He pauses. "You may finish," he says. And while their heads duck and they slurp the watery gruel, Father Ernst's mind wanders back to their first season below.

They had plenty of food in store—cobs stacked, kernels to pop or grind into grits and flour, wheat, nuts, grains, dehydrated fruit, sugar, canned fruit and vegetables, jams. Even fresh eggs from a few brown hens. He loved to spoon honey from the jar onto a slice of Mother Deborah's warm bread. He'd pull her yellow apron strings like horse reins and steer her onto his lap while he ate. Memaw Ruth, God rest her, sat beside him at the table head. All three pink and happy.

Mother Mary was ill but not yet dead. Susan pregnant with the twins. Rebekah was mirthful, not yet a wife, still sharing cots with the younger girls. There were apples in cold storage. Relish and pickles and tomato sauce and boxes of long, brittle spaghetti. The children would take noodles from the pot and fling them on the bunker walls where they'd stick and dry in shapes that sometimes looked like alphabet letters. Little hands painted them as decorations. After the paint dried, they'd spell out God's word until the letters crumbled and got swept up with the dust.

They used to throw those pieces away.

Father Ernst's favourite sermon—he still knows it by heart—never failed to rile up the women. The children would stamp and clap and sing. That's what the Family needs—inspiration.

Father Ernst looks about the Great Hall. Susan slumps, yawning. "Come, Mother Susan," he says. "Join us. I shall give a talk from the time before."

She looks at him queerly. He beckons. She sits, uncertainly, at his left hand. The coveted bride's place.

Father Ernst says, "Americans are overfed. Unused to honest work. They glutton themselves. Worship the false gods: fast food, television, money, and all of the seven deadlies."

The children gape. They don't know television. They've never seen money. He forgot that. He must revise.

"Cousins. We may feel pinched from time to time. We may remember something sweet and wish for it again—a milkshake or a piece of Memaw's pecan pie. My, wouldn't that tempt a sinner."

Susan looks aghast. Her hand shakes and drops to her lap.

"But we shall discover truths. Restricting junk food with all those intoxicating fats, those man-made poisons. That will give us years of living the rest of America will never have. We will be lean, spare, and alert."

Father Ernst looks at the blank, smudged faces around the table. Runny noses. Coughs erupt from concave chests; rounded bellies belie hunger. Beggarly waifs, every last one. Desperation fixes him. This was his best sermon; he toured the Midwest with it, hit the Deep South, town by town, on speaking tours—Louisiana, Alabama, Georgia, Mississippi, and South Carolina. He won conversions, lucrative donations, and powerful allies: Republican senators, gun lobbyists, ex-military. The CEO of an underground shelter company from El Paso County—that's who sent the architect to design their bunker, gratis. The man boasted, "If you can build a birdhouse, you can build one of our underground bomb shelters!" A like-minded former Homeland Securities official from Texas procured the retired nuclear weapons, rerouted weapons shipments. The Pentagon used to sell them on the quiet to townships that were convinced they were terrorists' targets. That man's strategic mind, his field experience, shaped the retribution plan they named The Great Standoff.

Father Ernst gestures to the girls' bench. The littlest one, whose name continually escapes him, sniffles. Ernst sees Memaw, Mary, and Deborah, smiling golden, cradling babies, sunlight in their fair hair. "Look at your Cousin Mothers. They are *all* your mother. How they glow," he says. "Look at their nurturing arms, full of children."

Then it's only Susan, humpbacked and dishevelled. Ruth and the twins, horrified.

Ernst shakes his head. Memaw was right here only a second ago. He's sure of it.

"Look at me, your one Father."

Here he would always stop and make fists. He would show his biceps and invite a child to run up from the audience to squeeze the hard muscle. The child would hang off his arm, and Father Ernst would lift and lower him like a weight. 'I'm strong, aren't I,' he would say, and the child would giggle. It always made the other children laugh, and that put parents at ease. 'I'm virile, aren't I, Mothers,' he would say, and his women would blush and nod. That often set the men on edge. But women in the congregation would also blush, wondering at so many satisfied wives.

Here and now. Heads nod around the wooden table. The youngest boy sleeps beside his bowl. The twins huddle for warmth. The sharp wings of their shoulders, their knobby spines, show through their shirts. Silas licks his spoon again and again. He sets it down with a clang. Susan stares into her lap, dismayed.

Father Ernst winds up for his big finale. How they used to cheer. "I am healthier now, happier here, with each one of you than ever before," he says, pointing into their dull faces. "I am just getting started. Mayhap I'll live forever!"

CHAPTER 15

Horizon splits. The deep pull of night releases its hold, and the sky begins to brighten. Paul stands and shakes off the stiffness in his limbs. He slings the rifle over his shoulder and resumes walking, leaning more heavily on his stick.

He has the cooked meat, wrapped. There are also the yucca leaves, the root that Susan can boil, and sage for tea. He dug up part of an enormous aloe, slit the juicy spike open with his knife, and ate one bite of the hydrating flesh. He wrapped the rest with the yucca. Memaw used to make an ointment for burns from this. It's enough food that Paul could return to the bunker, but he wants to scout the forest. If he's going to bring the girls up, he needs to know what is there, waiting.

The gas mask, clipped to his belt, swings with each step and thuds against his left thigh. His coveralls are unzipped at the neck and he pulls the UV hood off, for now. Scanning with the binoculars, he sees the green details of trees. Vultures still hover above the closest copse. Must be an injured animal. Something dying. Between himself and the trees are outcroppings of yucca, cacti, and sage. He will pick more on his return. The forest will also have food. Each season, Memaw took the children into the woods to teach them medicinal uses for plants, and which ones could be eaten. Evergreen needles, rich in vitamin C, make a strong tea. Amaranth, chickweed, clover, and dandelion are full of nutrients.

Mushrooms are tricky—easy to confuse. But summer berries, autumn nuts, burdock, and sunchokes—all good.

Paul needs a water source, and he should build a rough shelter. Ruth and Rebekah will be tired after crossing the sands. Abel and Leah. So tiny. And Susan's twins, taller but also weak. This is where the plan falls apart. He can't carry them all. But how can he leave them behind?

"It's not right," he told Rebekah.

"You have to choose," she said. "Be ruthless, or none of us will survive."

Now Paul wonders at her words. Did she mean he had to be *without Ruth*? Impossible. He took an oath, Rebekah knows this. He can't figure out an answer that will save them all. Ruth believes they must Ascend with Father Ernst. That way everyone leaves together. Wishful thinking. Different story if Father Ernst were out of the picture. Paul shakes this thought away and concentrates on simpler things.

What to bring from the bunker? Whoever comes, they'll need blankets. Knives—carbon steel blades hold their edge better than stainless steel—and a hacksaw and more of the plastic tarp. He pictures a small hut like the ones they built during summer campouts, structured around two large Y-shaped branches with a long ridgepole along the top. They'd lean leafy branches on either side for walls and fill the interior with leaves and forest debris for insulation. A place that Rebekah can guard while he and Ruth scout the white cliff beyond.

Weapons would help. Father Ernst has a secret stash—Paul remembers the men planning for every eventuality. Somewhere there is a serious military cache. The locked door to the kitchen pantry blends with the bunker walls, disguised against potential intruders. There used to be two pistols and an automatic rifle with ammunition hidden in there with the food, but those vanished with Thomas on his last topside mission. Paul has searched for a second false wall with hidden storage, to no avail. Father Ernst's chamber, always locked, is the only other place. Bad enough to break faith and escape. To trespass and steal from Father Ernst is a whole other thing. Back to that same problem—challenging Father Ernst. Paul wants to disappear peacefully, not fight.

Or does he? How many times has he awakened, dream hands wrapped around that bristling bearded neck? He has battled Father Ernst endlessly in his mind: grappled, punched, lynched, shot with a cross-bow, axe-hacked him to pieces. It's getting harder to tamp down his rage. Paul closes his eyes when the old man lifts a hand to the women; he counts to keep his calm—and has never made it past five. Instead, he intervenes and is beaten in their place. Locked up for Contemplation. Made an example of. It might be the real reason Father Ernst permits him to stay. So long as Paul voices his small resistance and is punished, no one else dares attempt it.

A sobering thought: *Am I standing in the way of their freedom?*

When Paul told Ruth the basic plan—to sneak away—she covered her ears. He didn't mention Rebekah. He pulled Ruth's hands apart to reason with her, and she hollered for him to "Act right! Abandoning Father Ernst and the Doctrine. For shame," she hissed. "Think of Memaw, how she'd weep."

He said, "We're dying, Ruth. Don't you see? Father Ernst has lost his way." She looked scared then, a child at last. She might have been crying but was too proud to let him see.

Paul's chest heaves, his breath comes shallow and his hands curl into fists. But he's got to keep a calm focus. He opens his mouth to relax his jaw. The closer the forest looms, the more vulnerable he is. If he gets there before noon, he'll rest in that deep shade, and save time not scrounging temporary shelter on the plain. It's sound. Smart. Yet the further on he walks, the stronger he feels a pull back to the bunker, as if he'd snagged a wool sweater and the whole knitted thing is unravelling behind him, yarn stretched out like guts. Dread pools in his belly. Mayhap the meat. Too rich?

The pastel horizon bleeds gold, and Paul remembers butter melting in Memaw's large skillet, topside, when he was just a boy. She'd crack eggs, three at a time, slop yolk and whites into the sizzle and scramble them with a fork. In this strangely blazing light, other memories surface too. The sun rises quickly, and after the golden blast there are other hues—silver and cream and the violet-blue trace just like Rebekah's veins at her wrists. Paul likes to gently thumb them, down to her buttoned sleeves, then imagine following the slender length of her arm to her shoulder, across her pale breast. This sunrise must be a sign. A promise. Rebekah's poem comes to him again. He'd wanted a keepsake—her handwriting on that delicate slip of quilting paper—but she said no. Instead, he had to memorize and recite the words until she was satisfied that he'd learned them, then eat the evidence while she watched him chew.

For Paul
Hush
It is best uttered like this and like this
A shy mouth and curious tongue
Your dark curls cupped in my trembling hands
Heated, alight
I come this night in silence
Words do not serve in this starless cathedral
So extend your quiet palms,
Accept this gift
Skin letters, our new alphabet,
Spill from our lips

Morning comes at him hard now. Paul pushes worry away, frees himself. He walks toward the glow, the ascending light of the eastern sky, and spreads his arms wide for Rebekah. Dawn is a new beginning, waiting just ahead.

CHAPTER 16

Rebekah will not get out of bed. The children gather round, murmuring their strange syllables, patting her shoulder. One combs and begins to braid her long hair. Why hasn't it fallen out, grief-stricken?

As a girl, summer humidity induced knotted rebellions at her crown and at the back, at her sweaty nape. "This hair has a mind of its own," Mother Deborah used to say, brushing and tsk-ing at the pouf of matted curls. There were tears and sometimes scissors fetched to cut out the worst bits.

Young Leah presses a dry mouth to Rebekah's waxen cheek. "I love you, Mother," she breathes into her ear, and Rebekah is undone.

"Get," she says, sharper than she intends, and the girls flee.

Silence again, at last.

But not quite. There are the sounds of the bunker itself: clanging in the pipes, the generator grumbling and humming, lights buzzing. Benches scrape the floor of the Great Hall when someone moves them. If she holds her breath, she can pick out urgent whispers, distant and ghostly. Susan and Ruth? Beyond the voices, the gentle growl and thud of cabinet drawers opening, shutting, the tin music of a hand stirring the cooking utensils, searching for a tool. Knife blade scraping against the sharpening steel. It must be Susan and Ruth in the kitchen, the air vent picking up sounds, carrying them aloft.

Rebekah and Paul sometimes met there in the night. Anyone awake in the women's chamber might have heard the telltale sounds:

hushed voices, zippers, cloth sometimes tearing in their haste. Reckless, pressed against the squat stove. She—lifted to the narrow counter, skirts and slip pushed up around her thighs; he suckling between. Rebekah, straddling him on the cold bare floor. She had to cover his mouth with her hand when he climaxed so as not to wake them all. If anyone had been listening, would they have let on by now? Once Susan discovered a pearlescent button from his shirt on the floor. She raised an eyebrow, more curious than accusing.

Some days, the only miracle Rebekah celebrates is that they have not yet been caught. Under the blankets, her fingers snake into her apron pocket. Two pills. She places one onto her dry tongue and swallows. The tablet sticks. She tries again. Now she sits up, swings her legs over the cot edge, shuffles to the showers. She plunges her cupped hands into the greasy basin and chokes back the grey water. Her parched tongue rejoices. Then it's just as miserable as before. She drinks again. The bitter aftertaste of lard soap turns her stomach, but she must keep this medicine inside. She gags and swallows, swallows. Peering into the warped mirror above the sink, Rebekah traces the pill's pathway with a fingertip, cracked lips down to chin, underneath into the shadows of her throat, the sharp collarbones. She loosens her dress, shrugs out of its long sleeves, stares at her rippled reflection.

Who am I?

Gaunt. Angular. Bulging eyes. Her mind almost turned to meanness. She looks like a praying mantis, the stick-legged insect that captured her childhood imagination because of the way it became its surroundings, invisible, a living secret camouflaged by grass. How it horrified her to learn that the female, post-coital, sometimes bites off the male's head. She has set Paul up for a similar death. Are they doomed to follow nature's brutal course? Not brutal. It is simply the turn of the wheel: dust to dust, seed to chaff.

There is a bad smell from the latrines again. Sometimes the toilets back up, and an ungodly stench fills the bunker. That alone could drive them topside, Rebekah hopes. Rebekah turns and, without fixing her dress, shambles back down the hallway to the women's chamber. She wants to lie down, be still. She steps out of the dress and, wearing only her rumpled slip, climbs back into the cot. She wants to blend faceless, nameless, invisible, into a lonesome field.

Today she is missing the sun, the sky, and most of all, the rich black earth. Tending the large gardens, delighting at her daily discoveries as plants mature and offer their bounty. Even turning the compost—hard work, smelly, not for the squeamish. Pitching straw, turning organic matter, rats sometimes scurrying, disturbed in their nests. She misses the complex aromatic layers: decaying produce mixed with the sweet soil. Sometimes a putrescence of liquid rot, a sure sign of imbalance—she would even miss that if they didn't get the occasional septic problem below. Early spring and late into fall, they would spread the fields with compost-enriched manure, and that heavy perfume declared itself all across the county. It clung to their hair and clothes. Manure caked their boots and could hardly be scrubbed from the stained knees of their work pants.

On their bi-monthly shopping trips, Rebekah remembers

townspeople sometimes holding their noses and drifting away from them, like they were lepers. One such trip—Rebekah was about nine, long after her accident and before her sister went completely wild—a boy hollered, "Stink Town, Stink Town," and his friends laughed, pointing. *Stink Town* was sprayed on road signs near their property in black paint, and twice drunken boys vandalized the church and the side of the barn. Her brothers would have beaten them, but that day, it was just Mother Deborah, Mary, Susan, and the girls. Rebekah's face burned with shame. Her sister marched over to the vandals, dragging Rebekah in her tightened grip. They could have been cousins, she and the town boys looked so much alike: pale, dirt-smudged, and freckled, with terrible teeth and vacant, almost cruel, blue eyes. The one who yelled looked unsure, possibly afraid of Rebekah's sister, who fairly vibrated with rage. His sneakers were worn thin, holes at the tips where his dirty toes poked through. The boys were no better in the stink department: musk and sweat and unwashed clothes laced with undertones of greasy chicken, boiled cabbage.

The standoff broke when her sister spat into one stunned face. Rebekah watched the frothy white spittle drip down the bridge of his turned-up nose. Then she was dragged by the wrist through the lot of them, into the air-conditioned grocery store behind. Bright lights made Rebekah blink. Her skin prickled with cold. Her sister strode to the taboo junk-food display rack, tore open a bag of Cheetos, and crammed handful after handful of the bright orange twists into her mouth while everyone watched. Silence, but for the song playing over the store speakers. Neil Diamond, her sister later said—how did she know? Gagging, still chewing, swallowing, stuffing more in, eyes watering, nose running, mixing with the orange crumbs that stained her face and fingers. Nobody stopped her. She threw down the empty bag and stalked out, past the disbelieving cashiers and lines of astounded shoppers, out into the parking lot and around the corner. Rebekah had to run to catch up. She found her in the alley, bending behind a dumpster, vomiting a great orange rush onto the asphalt.

Poor beautiful, brave Ezzie.

"Why do we have to be freaks?" she gasped. And a few minutes later, "Let's go home." She wiped the drool from her mouth with a sleeve.

Father Ernst roared when he heard. He whipped and locked her sister in the shed again. Pulled all of their teens from the local high school, claiming they could learn what they needed at home. He said, "Government lies and liberal thinking are ruining this great country, and I'll not contribute to America's demise." Henceforth, the girls studied domestic and culinary arts, plus herbal remedies with Memaw, animal husbandry with Susan, and beekeeping with Deborah. Compost and gardening was with Mary. The boys had other pursuits: barn and fieldwork, weaponry, machinery, working the generators and pumps, electrical and carpentry. Boys learned to build, and girls, to maintain.

From then on, only the men went into town. It wasn't a hardship, not really, since the rules softened whenever they left. Memaw opened the church windows and played piano for hours, everything in her repertoire. Picnic lunches were made from leftovers, and the children ran wild. In summer, the women stripped down to their slips and lay in the sunny yard like cats. One rainy day, Mary brought the forbidden box from hiding—a small black-and-white television with spindly antennae. She plugged it in and they crowded around, cooing and clapping. They watched a cat and mouse cartoon that Memaw remembered from her childhood—*The Tom and Jerry Show*—agape, completely transported, and then a remake featuring Pépé Le Pew, a skunk in heat hounding a small black cat. Memaw turned it off. "Nothing funny about being chased by a Tom," she said, and that was that. No more secret talking box.

The pills draw Rebekah, laced in memory, deeper into dreamland. The Farm, the Family, dissipates. She is in a forest, lush and green, filled with barrel-trunked trees so wide her arms reach only partway around. They are as big as a house. Bigger. So tall that the sky is obliterated by the leafy canopy above. Paul stands among them. In this vision, he is older, a grown man, filled out in torso and across his stooped shoulders. Grey at the temples. He looks strong yet weary. Still handsome. Beside him stands a woman, a warrior bride, a rebel with startling black eyes. Branches twist around them and disappear into a thousand shades of green. Roots and branches entwine, equally buried in the rich loamy earth and in the starlit heavens above.

Rebekah wakes with a dull knowing. He will belong to another some day. And she has no right to bring more children into this miserable existence, into their legacy of hate and shame. If it is a boy, sweet and soulful like Paul, he will be made to pay for their sins. And if a girl? Rebekah can only weep at the thought.

In the new world, there will be no time for quilting. No time for making bread and shucking corn, for grinding it into flour and grits. This place will be fast-moving and dangerous, like a river's lethal current. No room for nostalgia or hesitation. There will be only the things a person can carry on her back and in her heart, in her mind. She will need to run, run, and keep running, in order to survive.

CHAPTER 17

A fierce chill seizes their bedroom, one Ruth cannot shake, not even with another shawl wrapped around her. Susan, called by Father Ernst for the first time in over a year, will at least appreciate the warmth of his chamber, something Hannah boasts about. "It's spacious, Cousin Ruth, and heated—you can't imagine!" Still, Ruth pities Susan. Apprehension sparked her otherwise dim eyes and slowed the drag of her foot as she approached his beckoning hand. And Hannah—so used to Father's comforts—will be bitter, still locked in the wintry cell for Contemplation.

Rachel and Helen and Leah curl in their cots. Ruth settles an extra quilt over each one. These nights, they fall asleep so abruptly that Ruth feels compelled to check for a fluttering pulse. They slumber right through. No more crying and shuffling to a mother bed for comfort. Mornings, Susan must rouse them brutishly. And when they wake, they speak of dreams—vivid, intoxicating dreams that rob them of rest.

Rebekah, mute and pale, still lies prone. Ruth touches her forehead: pallid and cold. "Wake up," Ruth says.

Nothing.

"Wish you'd talk. I've a need."

Rebekah doesn't move.

"Well, I shall speak and hope you hear me. Father Ernst is set for me to marry. What can I do?"

If only Paul were here. The bunker is so much worse without him, and without Rebekah's gentle grace buffering them all. Ruth stifles a sob.

Rebekah's hand twitches. It clamps hard on Ruth's wrist. Slowly, Rebekah turns her head toward Ruth. Her eyes are so dilated, pupil swallows iris. She shakes her head back and forth. Nothing but air gasps out of her open mouth.

"Mama." A hushed voice at the door.

Ruth turns. Abel, barefoot, has a large wet spot on his rumpled pyjama pants. He's pissed himself again.

"What now. Whyn't Silas help you?"

The child says nothing, just shivers.

Ruth wrenches her wrist free from Rebekah's cold grip. She strokes Rebekah's unsettled face, tries to soften her expression. "I'll be back," she says.

She walks Abel to the showers and helps him strip. Ribs point like fingers, front and back, and a hard potbelly pushes below. Ruth pulls clean towel and cloth from the cupboard, and he gives over his soiled clothing. The pyjamas reek of urine. Ruth pictures herself red-knuckled and whip-sore, trying to scrub that smell out in the cold basin. They've so little left, they reuse the dish and laundry water—icy grey with floating lard-soap slivers.

"May as well burn them to keep warm."

"Oh."

"Don't tell no one," she says. "I mean it." She balls the cotton up tight and, instead of adding it to the laundry bin, sets it aside.

The child smiles once, quickly. "Nobody will know I had an accident?"

"Not if we burn the sheets too," she says. A plan forms. She has other evidence to dispose of.

Ruth wipes Abel's bare skin with a cloth. He shivers. She dunks and wrings out the rag, wipes again at his bottom.

"Who helps you bathe?"

"Mother Rebekah but now she's sick."

Ruth sucks her teeth. "Next time come get me. I'll help."

"You're a girl."

"Not really. I'm Ruth."

She towels him dry and helps him into a clean pair of flannels with feet, a trap door, and snaps all up the front. "Still cold?"

He nods.

She layers another set over top and holds his feet between her blistered hands to warm them. "Now we've got to strip the bed. Put on new sheets. Are the boys awake?"

He shrugs. If Ruth is caught in the boys' room there will be more to "contemplate." Her palms can't take the willow again.

"Come. You're sleeping in our room."

"No girls!"

"In a clean bed by yourself."

Abel looks stricken. But what else can she do? It will be fine, as long as Susan stays the night with Father and does not find out. Ruth takes his hand. "Okay?"

"Okay."

In the women's chamber, Ruth turns back the bedclothes on an unused cot. Abel crawls in.

"Smells better here," he says.

"I should hope so. Goodnight."

"Goodnight, Mother."

Ruth's chest heats. A bubble rises inside, trapped.

Back in the showers, alone, Ruth drops her grimy trousers and peels off woollen socks that hold their shape on the floor. She piles the bloody rag, formerly her underpants, with Abel's soiled pyjamas. She dips a fresh cloth in the grey-water bucket and begins to wash her lower half. She must wet and wring out the cloth several times before her skin is clean. She adds this stained rag to the burn pile. Ruth's knees knock from the cold. She pulls on clean cotton underpants, woollen tights, and an extra pair of socks, then folds a clean, dry washcloth inside the crotch of the underpants to soak up her sorrow.

Another rag submerged; she tracks her steps, wiping at every smudge, balling the cloth tight when she's done. Now that her lower half is clean and clothed, she sets about washing the rest. Her sweater and shirt go in the laundry bin. She sponges her underarms, small breasts, and narrow torso. She scrubs her hands, fingers, and thin arms, and reaches the cloth around her prominent ribs, the back of her neck, behind her ears. Her teeth chatter. Goose bumps dimple her blueing skin. She pulls on an undershirt with long sleeves. Next, she finds a fresh nightshirt in the cupboard. She wraps a flannel blanket around her shoulders like a shawl, and gathers the dirty clothes.

The Great Hall is unlit. A pale glow spills from underneath Father Ernst's door. He's running lights, a heater, and who knows what else while the rest of them freeze. Ruth enters the small kitchen and realizes, too late, that the gas is off and so is the ventilation. There will be no burning anything tonight, not without making some noise or filling the Hall with smoke. Abel's pyjamas will have to wait. But she cannot risk her blood tide discovery. The Family hardly produces garbage, so she can't put it there. Every item is scrutinized for repurposing. Even the most useless-seeming things are categorized and put in containers in the main pantry. Old food bins now house rusty nails, bolts, broken springs, ballpoint pen canisters, buttons, broken zippers, pieces of shoelace.

Ruth has another idea. She unlocks and rolls open the tunnel door. Shuts it behind her. Her breath hangs in the air like tiny clouds. She feels her way down the frigid tunnel until the bare pulse of the cairn light shows itself. There's nothing else in the dark, not one scuttling rat. "Forgive me, God. Forgive me, Memaw," she says before dismantling the cairn, one palm-sized rock at a time. She buries her blood-stained clothes inside. Then she restacks the stones.

Ruth prays, "Holy Father in Heaven, forgive this unclean body, this silence, these lies. How heavy, my burden. Shine Your light on Paul wheresoever it finds him, and bring him home. Send us a sign for the Ascension, God, I beg you. Amen."

Retracing her steps, she slides open the tunnel door and closes it carefully, sending the bolt home. She tiptoes past Father Ernst's door over to where Hannah sits huddled on the cousin board, knees drawn to her chin, arms wrapped around her shins.

"Hannah."

The girl's watchful eyes are open. Ruth unwraps the flannel blanket from her own shoulders and hands it between the bars. "I know how cold it gets here."

Hannah doesn't move. She says, "Usurper!"

"What for now?" says Ruth.

"I seen your blood in the bucket. You let Father alone."

"Hannah, take this. Don't be silly."

She snatches the blanket from Ruth. Wraps it tightly around herself. "It's *my* time. I'm the bride," she mutters.

"Then don't tell anyone," says Ruth.

Hannah's eyes narrow on Ruth. "Keep your womanhood secret?"

"I wish you would."

Hannah sits back onto the cousin board, blanketed and smug. "Well. Bring me my woollen leggings and the soft green sweater, and I'll think about it."

CHAPTER 18

Father's chamber is warm and bright. Susan swept and mopped it earlier. She wiped the sooty dust from the walls, taking down each framed photograph to dust carefully and remount in order: Memaw, Deborah, and Mary—sun-soaked on the main porch so many years ago. Then Deborah's handsome boys, just before they were martyred in Washington. Third, Mary's eldest sons, pinned with the Family's insignia. They carried out the Atlanta and Cincinnati attacks. Next, twelve dark-suited men encircling a white-robed Father Ernst—ministers from the sister Families. God knows if they're still similarly bunkered, eking out survival. Father Ernst lost contact—no more internet or cellphone service—after going to ground.

Last, Susan's favourite picture. A black-and-white photo of the farm, featuring the main house and barn with the church spire behind, the ridge breaching the orchard, and fields rippling beyond. The light is peculiar. Daybreak mist pulls like wraiths from the gnarled fruit trees and from the rows of tousled cornstalk. Susan hears phantoms—beasts lowing, hens clucking, and children hand-clapping their songs on the church steps. She traces a silver spiral up, up to the edge of the frame with her finger.

"Come," says Father Ernst from the doorway. He turns the bolt and strides to his chair on the other side of the room.

The bed is luxurious. Susan put the wine-coloured flannels on just the other day. High thread-count cotton pillowslips—worn, but still slick to the touch. Father Ernst's blankets are woollen blends lined with satin—store-bought, not made by the women like the ones tucked into their own cots. Susan stoops to straighten Father's slippers and to flip back the corner of the oval rag-tied rug she made from strips of disused clothing. She had used an old toothbrush, removing its head and filing the handle to a rough needlepoint, looping thread through the hole at the other end. Easier on the wrists, and what else were they to do with all those chewed-down toothbrushes? The rug is well made. Not beautiful, not like his mail-order blankets, but it's serviceable and keeps the chill off his feet.

"Sit," he says, patting the wide bed.

Susan slowly lowers her haunches. Pain shoots up the left hip and knots like an angry ball in her left foot. She leans to the right and breathes heavily. "Setting's not the joy you'd imagine," she says, by way of apology.

"What's better for you?" he asks gently.

"On my side."

"Go ahead."

Susan stretches out, draws her leaden legs onto the mattress and sighs. Her back is to Father Ernst. She'd much prefer to keep her eyes on him, but the threat of rolling over and inciting a paroxysm of pain subdues her. Firestorms run the length of her spine.

She had her initial episode the day they descended. The Family was bunkered safely when the first wave hit: twelve synchronized blasts carried out by the disciples in as many cities. As predicted, immediately following the explosions, thousands of cellphones snapped into simultaneous use—emergency calls mostly, but also the panic-stricken calling of loved ones—and those frequencies unwittingly set off a second round of explosives. Below ground, the Family listened to frenzied updates on the Ham radio and watched the radiation monitor. Susan began to tremble. Had they really done this terrible thing? Father Ernst, the great mastermind, crouched on his divan, radiated with a kind of jubilant madness. Then—somewhat unexpected—aftershock in each of the cities, the thermal pulse invoked noxious fires that burned along desolate, rubble-filled streets near the original bombsites. Gas stoves lit for dinner in the Midwest time zone became tertiary explosives, cutting a swath of destruction through thousands more homes, doubling the death toll. After that, fallout drifted in a steady north-easterly path from each site along clogged freeways, while hysterical families tried to flee. Within an hour, the whole world knew—dirty bombs had targeted ten American and two Canadian cities within minutes of each other. Newsmen called it "an unprecedented and unfathomable act of terrorism"; at first, they blamed the Middle East, much to Father Ernst's disgust. His press statement, emailed one day before the scheduled blasts, had been dismissed as the ravings of a lunatic.

Susan fell reeling to the bunker floor, and the Family held hands around her while she seizured. They chanted and sang, and Father Ernst spoke in tongues. Susan had hoped, while in the throes of her affliction, that the news coverage, that this strange Family ritual, was merely a figment of her illness. But when she finally came to, lying on the cement floor in a soiled dress with a bleeding, swollen mouth, she learned the truth. News reports of FBI raiding some of the other settlements, dismantling their bunkers, and shooting or imprisoning their members, sent Father Ernst spiralling into despair. They were traitors, enemies of the state, once and for all.

Here, now, in Father Ernst's chamber, Susan shakes her head to clear these memories. It won't do to think on the past. Never does.

"Susan, we must talk about the Family. There is a spiritual deficit haunting us just now. Have you noticed?" Father Ernst's voice is somewhere between intimate and sermonizing. Conspiring, but still instructing.

Her shoulders tense. She stares at the wall in front of her, blank and cold. "What do you mean, Father?"

"The children are listless. The women are ragged. There is no joy here, and I fear we are losing sight of our purpose. Do you agree?"

Does he want her to agree? Then he can't backtrack. But if she disagrees, she's contradicting him.

"Father, what do you want me to say?"

"The truth, of course. What you observe. What you think is the problem."

A coal heats inside her. It burns to white ash. What she thinks is of no interest to anyone.

She says, "I just do the cleaning."

Father Ernst exhales an irritated sigh.

Susan considers the effort of sitting up, turning to face him—

white hairs escaping nostrils and ears to join the rush of moustache and beard, wild to the belly, the sometimes hint of lip inside all that hair when he talks or laughs or shouts, the barbaric tufts of hair above his eyes, and cheekbones that sharpen his face, as though a drawstring tightens behind his head, pulling the skin taut. Under his watery eyes, the soft pouches of yellowing skin.

No. Susan prefers how he used to look. Tall and slim and clean-shaven. Bookish. Often contemplative. Nothing at all like the men she grew up around.

"I'm waiting, Mother." His voice is laced with annoyance.

Susan's body stiffens. She must tread lightly or this shall end poorly. Memaw knew how to handle his moods. That woman could settle a torrid bull.

"Ernst," she says at last. "We're starving. That's the problem."

The chamber is a hushed tomb.

"Tell me more."

"That's it. Can't hardly sing or pray, they're too weak."

"And?"

"And?" Susan licks her cracked lips.

"What else," he says, encouraging.

"Well, there's naught left in the oats bin. The water's too low. We've only the wafts of fuel." Susan feels relief, unburdening these worries at last. "What shall we do? The children are malnourished. I can hardly get the chores done alone. These girls, they don't know how to work. Too soft."

"What, pray tell, do you recommend?"

"Oh, that's not for me to decide."

"Certainly it is. So many problems. What's the answer?"

"Well, Father ..." Susan licks her lips again. "I'd say we'd likely need to go topside. Before—"

"Before what, Mother?" Father Ernst's voice is solid, thick with emotion.

She hears it now. "Before it's too late," she whispers.

"Get up."

She whimpers. Tricked again.

Susan presses weight into her hands, pushes up despite the pain, and swings heavy feet back to the floor. She slowly stands and steadies herself with the mattress. She dare not look at him.

"What divine influence informs your opinion?" Father Ernst enunciates crisply.

"Father, I beg you, don't mock me."

"Does God Himself come to you with insight?"

"Heavens, no. I never said that."

"You said the girls are soft, the children weak, the water and food all gone." Father Ernst spits as he shouts. "You said we should leave this haven!" His neck strains and his eyes are wild.

Susan clasps her hands. "Forgive me."

"We shall not Ascend until I have completed the seventh. Until I have a worthy tribe to offer. Until God comes to me Himself!"

Susan whispers her prayer. How will this rage pass? She knows. A beating. A despoiling. A sermon. Or, his favourite, a combination of the three—a punishment performance that will extinguish her puny fire within. "I only said what I know, what's plain. I don't pretend to be nothing special."

The blow comes, exacting and pitiless. Her bad leg buckles on the carpet. She lands hard. Cries out. Her back spasms. An agony writhes through her left side. She cannot fend him off. She's trapped, curled on the rug, and Father Ernst looms above.

CHAPTER 19

Morning comes and Susan is not in her cot. Ruth forces herself to sit up. She rubs her eyes until the blurry beds come into focus. There is a pain chipping at her skull, needling her scalp, making it hard to think. Her mouth is very dry. Morning. The hard fast.

Ruth should wake the children. She moves stiffly in the cold room. She shouts and claps. Nothing. Ruth swallows panic and shakes Helen by the shoulders. The girl's eyes roll.

Then, "You're hurting me."

"Scared me." Ruth straightens Helen's nightgown and bed sheets. She lowers herself on the girl's cot. She rubs her eyes again.

"It was wonderful," whispers Helen. "My dress was purple and red and I had gold jewellery with stones and pearls. I sat upon a red horse, and I was in charge of everything. I had piles of gold and slaves to do my bidding."

"The Whore of Babylon," says Ruth. "Don't say nothing about that to no one."

"Is it the Devil?" Helen frowns.

"Mayhap."

"Oh, what will I do?"

"Pray, I suppose," says Ruth.

"I will. I'm hungry."

"I know."

"Will we eat today?"

Ruth shakes her head. "Hard fast," she says.

Helen falls back to the mattress. "Can't we just stay? Mother Rebekah does."

"She's sick and you're not. Get dressed. Lots of layers. We got the Sit today, so try and keep warm. Help me wake the cousins?"

Helen shakes Rachel, and the two of them rouse Leah.

"What's Abel doing here? He's a boy."

"None of your business," says Ruth. "Wash faces and hands and get dressed. Take Abel with you." Mothering, it seems, has come upon her with or without the bridal contract. For once she is glad there is no meal to prepare. She can't do it all on her own. But poor Susan has been, she realizes.

After Ruth helps the children dress, she hovers near Rebekah. A foul odour blooms. No one helped her to the latrine, and Ruth can't bear to clean this right now. She can't think for the pain in her head. Regrettably, Rebekah will have to wait.

One note swells and fills the bunker. It rattles her ribs. She has not yet toileted or checked her blood rag. A dress. She must wear a dress or she will provoke Father's ire again. Ruth rifles through Rebekah's under-bed storage box. "You won't mind," she mutters. Rebekah's new quilt is folded and stacked on top of her other things. Finished, at last. Ruth finds the worn blue dress and yanks it out. She drops the bodice and skirt over her regular long-sleeved shirt and trousers. It hangs long at the sleeves and hem. Sags at the chest. The waist has been let out recently, a strip added to each side, so it fits over the lumps of Ruth's belt and knife pouch. She is not ready to give up the hunt yet. Who, other than Paul, can procure? Silas thunders about like a forest boar. He is adept at Scriptures and peddling the generator but little else.

Paul. Where in God's light might he be? His name is a tumbling rock, a landslide, and Ruth pinches herself to stop the rush of feeling.

"Come back," she whispers. "Please."

In the Great Hall, the others are already sitting cross-legged. A bedraggled crew, for certain. Hannah, released from Contemplation, faces the Family beside Father Ernst. Wrapped in a thick robe, she frowns, looking vaguely victimized whenever Father Ernst glances at her and vindicated when he looks away. She sits upon the red Vestal Cushion, declaring her moon time, which bodes well for Ruth and their secret. Cousin brides need not fast like the rest, else they might never conceive. So Hannah lifts her favourite cup and sips noisily, then sets it back down. Each time she reaches for her cup, Ruth and the children lean forward, licking their parched lips. When Ruth makes eye contact with her, Hannah shrugs as if to call her a fool.

The Great Hall used to have a warmth that lingered well into the Sixth and Seventh. Cousin mothers baked bread and slow-cooked stews throughout the other days. They'd bulk up on the fifth—complex carbohydrates and whole grains that digested slowly, helping to keep them going through the fasts. The Sixth was a day of tonics and vitamin supplements. Once it felt good and right to restrict meals each week. Like their insides were getting a cleaning. And in that quiet time on the Seventh, when they sat neighbour to neighbour, they shared a great aloneness and awaited God's command. Ruth looked forward to it. The Hall was full of mothers and cousins, and when they hummed and chanted and held the one note together, she could feel her mind begin to open to God's Holy outpouring.

Today Father Ernst sits on the Holy Dais. He strikes the dinner bell with a tiny stick, a different sound than their regular call to meals. Lights flicker. Will Silas break the Sit and power the stationary bike instead? That would be a first. But if they sit in darkness, when God Himself peers down below the blackened earth to gift his visions, how will He see Father Ernst and know with whom to break bread?

Father Ernst says, "Observe your breath, in and out. Release hate, release fear, release doubt. Release hunger, there is none. Release thirst, it is a lie. Release all pain from your body, for that is Satan's false body. There is no resistance. Open wide the mind. Hollow the heart."

Release Paul. But she cannot. He is lodged inside. The lonesome dregs of his memory grip her and shall never be hastened away. Ruth closes her eyes and breathes in time with the others. In and out. The sound of air inhaling and exhaling is a gentle surge. "Like the ocean," Memaw used to say, but Ruth has never heard the ocean. Never seen it, not even in a picture.

Ruth peeks. The children in front of her are on their way to trance with dropped shoulders, slack mouths. The twins sway in gentle orbits upon their crossed legs. Abel slumps against Silas, who pushes him up, but the little boy shudders an exhale and falls again. Silas sits tall, rigid. There is a rattling in his congested lungs—a rasping louder than the others'—that would have Rebekah worrying with ointments and a poultice if she were feeling more herself. If they still had medical supplies. Beyond Silas, a misshapen figure broods in the corner. It's Susan, more humped and dispirited than usual, almost unrecognizable.

There's no real work on the Seventh, just the task of sitting still and not falling asleep while they're meant to be visioning. The hardest part is not allowing the mind to wander and hook itself into the Devil's fertile fantasies. Ruth closes her eyes again. She breathes deeply and tries to loosen her mind to unite with the Family. She likes to picture a warm quilt unrolling over them all, blanketing them with calm and quiet. But today it's as though the rest have gone ahead down a country road and she cannot catch up. Her abdominal pain ramps up, and she can hardly stop thinking of water. Of food. Of the last thing that passed her lips—a cube of Father's sugar. She falls farther behind the others with each breath. An image of Paul receding in the opposite direction chains her, anchored.

Father Ernst chimes the bell again. Now they sing the one note. A sustained chord warms the air. Usually Ruth loves to let sound fill her belly and chest, pour out her mouth in song. Today she feels detached. Hopelessness swells. Ruth joins in with an involuntary sob.

"You are God's soldiers," says Father Ernst.

"One Family, God's army," they say.

"You are the future.

"We are the lambs. We follow His command."

Ruth does not feel like a soldier. She is cold, famished, and her knees bruise on the concrete. Her belly rolls with pain, and wetness spots the crotch of her underthings—more blood. She wants a blanket, a biscuit, a mother. Now that womanhood is at her doorstep, she tastes fear—metallic, like the rust of an old spoon.

Father Ernst's footsteps grow louder. His smell is powerful, close.

"Kneel." His voice comes from above. His hand rests on Ruth's head. She moves like water in a bucket, her arms slop and hang at her sides. "Pray," he says.

She brings hands underneath her chin, palms together. Should she open her eyes? He'll think she's inviting the Devil's idle thoughts. Her breath comes ragged.

"Pray," he insists.

Ruth says, "God in Heaven, watch over the Family. Shine Your light upon us and keep us safe. Amen."

Father's robe brushes against her clasped hands. His feet straddle either side of her knees. Heat comes off him like a small fire, and his pungent smell fills her nose—sour, with a strong hint of latrine. Ruth listens to deep inhalations and the slow air unfolding—the Family breathing as one. Except for Father, whose hot snorts blow on her chastened hair. And except for Ruth, whose eyelids pinch out a single rolling tear when he finally steps away.

Minutes are hours, hours a season. The Hall grows colder, darker.

Words echo and subside. Ruth's knees ache, then burn beyond feeling. Her limbs tingle and go numb. Her face is stone, but inside, her mind veers. It plunges unbidden, submerges thousands of leagues below.

Memories—her birth father, now traitor, toasting contraband marshmallows for Ruth and Paul through the open door of their woodstove. The smell, burnt sugar, the crisp bubbled outer skin and gooey pull of the molten insides. A mug of hot cocoa. And, like a shock from the frayed generator cord, she recalls a wet nose nuzzling her neck, snuffling her ear, a dog's tongue lapping sticky crumbs from the corner of her mouth. Their dog. Warm fur—enough to bury Ruth's face in. Ears that stood at any far-off sound, a tail that whip-whip-whipped, then curled to his own nose in sleep.

Oh! she nearly says aloud.

Their whitewashed log cabin with creaking veranda and garden out back. The purple flowers that flourished each spring. That happy, safe past slams into her. Ruth pushes each picture away, just as they've been taught. She clears her mind. Imagines a zero, a sphere of nothing. But the thread of memory is stitched deep in Ruth's body. It circles her bones and pulls, old truths knotted in time.

CHAPTER 20

Paul creeps through forest shadows. It is disorienting, this old growth and needle-dropped carpet. Twigs and branches crackle underfoot. Foliage closes in, and his shoulders hunch. Wary sets of eyes follow, he's sure—but when he whirls to look, there is only pine and sapling, brush and soil. He wants a perch with a vantage point, someplace hidden. If he were stronger, he'd climb a great tree. Instead he must make do with a hollow under a thick bush of understory covered in ropey wisteria. He stick-prods matted leaves, checking for copperheads and cottonmouths and black widow spiders before nestling in.

Sunspots dapple the green. He breathes earth and moss and pine, a hint of decay. Mosquitoes swarm, buzzing his ears, landing on his neck and face to bite. He pulls on the UV hood to keep them at bay. As his body stills, the forest noises distinguish themselves, layered and distinct. Birds trill their call-and-response. Leaves dance the breeze, shimmying. Something scampers in the overhanging branches—grey squirrel or opossum? Bobcats are unlikely. Intermittent shedding of twigs and nuts and animal droppings thud on the mulchy forest floor. Everything around him sings, alive.

He lifts the UV hood to drink from the canteen. It's getting low and must be refilled. Somewhere an underground river bubbles up in the heart of these woods, forming a pool that feeds the forest. Years ago, they came to fish and hunt here, and Paul's dad explained how the natural caverns in the bedrock had been weakened by oil drilling that sucked the county dry, and by the mining companies decades earlier. The result—underground chambers could shift and buckle. During flash floods and in spring thaw, they filled with water, which seeped through the ground. The pool sometimes spilled over, begetting a slough like the marsh at the base of the white cliffs.

But the Big Drought changed all that. Dramatic drops in the water table meant that topsoil was no longer supported and the underground caverns could collapse, giving way to sinkholes at the surface. No warning—the earth would simply open its maw and swallow itself whole. The forest was also shrinking. Each year, the outer stand of dead and dying trees with desiccated understory grows; the hot sands and lethal winds erode it endlessly, driving moisture from branch and soil alike. If Paul lights a campfire, he must tend it carefully.

He chews another small piece of meat, thinking about the hare's sacrifice and his remorse for taking another life, however hungry he is. Once they settle in the forest, they can focus on plant-sourced food; they can stop all this killing. Paul sends his pledge skyward, beyond darkened treetops, to the imagined hearts and minds of all the earth's creatures. How will they cultivate land without seeds? Rebekah confessed that she and Susan, in desperation, had broken into the seed bank months ago. Many samples were already ruined due to a faulty moisture guard. They rinsed and sprouted the rest in dark cupboards and quietly fed them to the children, a few at a time. Father Ernst still doesn't know. They will have to collect and store fresh seeds their first year above ground and forage in the meantime. Tricky, but it can be done.

Paul is ready to move. He stuffs the UV hood and gas mask into the food pack and strings it out of reach by knotting a rope around it and throwing the other end over a thick branch. He pulls the loose end, hoisting the pack high in the air, then weights the loose rope end with a rock. Leaves the throwing stick at the base of the tree. He keeps the rifle, his knife, the canteen. The half-crushed can is in his pocket, in case.

He steps lightly, but he's sure the whole forest hears this intrusion. It's darker; the overhead canopy thickens. Wisps of spiders' webbing catch and pull on his face. Sticky threads stream behind as he makes his way deeper. A woodpecker shadows him for a while, gliding to low-hanging branches and onto stumps that he drills for ants or beetles. Paul can't take his eyes from the scarlet flash at the crown and bold pattern on the body feathers. *Magnificent.* The woodpecker swoops to a fallen log, attacking it. It looks directly at him, then hops down behind the log. When Paul steps closer, the bird pops up and laughs that ridiculous call. It glides farther and hides. Pops up again, and they both laugh.

Silence descends. The woodpecker startles. It flies up, away from the trees, is gone. Paul looks around. He's off course—got distracted following the bird. Everything is changed since he last camped out. Lost people tend to circle in the direction of their dominant hand, no matter how convinced they've followed a straight line. He can try looping backwards, veering to his left. Cursing himself, he pats the coveralls, hoping for a compass in one of the pockets. He doesn't normally rely on one, but he's got no time to waste wandering.

Shooka-shooka-shook. That unholy rattle. Paul scans the ground around him, back and forth, and cannot locate it. Peering over his shoulder, he catches the swaying head of a pit viper—tongue flicking, grey body coiled. The black v-shaped crossbands and raised black tail confirm it's a rattler. Too long for a pygmy, and without the tell-tale patterns of the eastern diamondback, the most dangerous snake in America. Probably a timber rattler—venomous, but generally less prone to attack. Paul licks his lips. His old fear grips him. He fights the panic rising in his belly and, still crouching, shifts his weight imperceptibly. He backs away carefully, giving it a wide berth. He'll have to leave the kit and the Ruger for now.

Sweat stands on Paul's upper lip. It beads along his hairline, itching its way down his face. The black vertical eye slits unnerve him, and when it hisses, the viper's bared fangs repel. Paul springs to one side and in that same instant the rattler explodes its full length. It falls short. Paul scrambles to the other side of a fallen log. The snake coils to strike again but Paul scuttles away, keeping a safer distance between them.

Standing tall, Paul presses himself against the sturdy trunk of a spruce pine. Gradually his breath steadies, his pulse slows. He watches the snake's head sway, its tongue dart, scenting the air for danger. Paul's canteen remains within the rattler's reach, the Ruger lies beside it. He could die without them. He's still got the knife at his belt. Paul's toes tingle, go numb, but he must wait. His muscles tremor. Still, he cannot draw his gaze from the large snake. When it begins its retreat, Paul marvels at its supple movements, black markings inching forward, fluid, full of grace. It crosses the clearing, camouflages itself with the forest floor and disappears entirely.

His mother's voice fills his head: *They deserve a life, too.*

Paul exhales deeply. This was a close call. He stretches his limbs to dispel the adrenaline, and returns to the clearing for his things.

Thwack. He hears it too late. Identifies the source, dumbly. An arrow, embedded through the canteen's strap, neatly landed between his outstretched hands. He could have lost a finger, could have been crucified through either palm. Instinct kicks in, and he dives over the dead log again, flattens himself in the fallen leaves for cover. The Ruger, lost to him now. Canteen, pinned to the clearing floor. He can't quiet the blood pumping in his ears. The attacker only has to come at a slight angle for an open shot. There could be more than one; he could be surrounded. Paul strains for footsteps and hears nothing. A shimmy of overhead branches. He tilts his chin, looks up.

Not squirrels, after all. The quivering bow, a cocked arrow aimed true, and a set of dark eyes squinting right at him.

CHAPTER 21

It is time.

Rebekah worships the sun, the stars, the waterways, and all the great mysteries of the universe. Through a glint of the needle's eye lies a passage, and she will float there, she will sink there, she will come.

Rebekah is in the river, dress soaked and heavy as a grain bag, fabric sucking at her thighs, scratching her wet skin. She wades deeper, deeper until her feet cannot touch and she begins to kick. Her apron billows wide and weightless, air trapped under, puffing it up. She is free, so free. Arms outstretch to the tiny suck of toothless fish, feet churn to keep her afloat. Water rushes like voices—fairy music—and wind sets all the leaves above her to dance. The pale green shoots of cattails whistle and bend. Sunlight dazzles the river's surface: diamonds, heaps of them, everywhere she turns. Below are bottom dwellers, whiskery cat fish, mud-wallowing creatures in the shadows. Beyond that, moon-coloured river stones beckon from the murky bed.

She follows them.

This river runs the length of the Farm acreage. The current is swift. It fills roadside ditches and flows out past the orchard bluffs where it swerves and snakes back, and abruptly disappears into the hallowed ground. Sinkhole. Water rushes there, determined, and so does she. Into this womb, this secret opening, past the bones and the stones of the ancestors, into the earth's own den. Now she is carried into the abyss, wet and cold and lost to all that she loves.

She is twirling the whirlpool tide, sucked under, mouth full of water, lungs on fire. Her body bangs against the subterranean rock. She is thrown, bruised and wanting. She bobs to the surface, eyes wide and beyond terror. She is caught on the shale. Water streams her gasping face. What is this place? She is in an underground cavern, down among the fossils and cavefish and the secretive troglobites. A round, midnight pool—she knows it from her dreams. Blue-black reflections on the rock walls lit by a finger of sun that spears a prehistoric fissure above, pointing down, down, light years from its source. Here, among the drippings and splashings, lurks something unnamed, something fearsome and older than the earth itself. What is it? She could stay here, creep onto a sharp abutting ledge and cling to it with all her strength. But what for? What manner of life or non-life will embrace her when she finally can no longer keep her grip on the rock?

She releases.

She doesn't believe in God anymore. Only in the Mother, the land of the Mothers—the Dreamtime, where all is revealed to the watchful eye.

Now the river runs colder, faster. Far ahead there is another small opening: golden daylight. She knows where it will resurface, where she must go—this time for keeps. This is how she'll enter the Garden. Not through the locked and guarded front gates, but on her own terms, in her own time. Up the river with the fishes to safely beach on the sun-drenched shore under the glorious canopy of the forest, where she shall embrace them at last: the mothers, the babies, each of the betrayed dogs. There, in the meadow, in the wild and tangled grass, will she lie down to rest. There will Paul find her someday, waiting.

Birds call and roost in the wild understory. Foxes leap the tall grass. Bears follow the bees and hunker down at water's edge. In the centre of the mystical woods, this river is life, feeding and cleansing and endlessly carrying away. She has become it, now. It is kin. She is in the river, of the river—the eternal rushing to an unknown sea.

CHAPTER 22

When the end bell chimes, Susan opens and closes the fingers of one hand. The left is locked in an arthritic spasm. Children stagger up and huddle for warmth. They shake limbs, massage sensation back into feet and calves.

Susan wants her own cot. She wants a bath, a fresh slip. She needs looking after, and there is no one to tend her wounds. Her face is puffed, hot. She cannot find her way to standing. Her joints are too stiff.

Hannah's long robe sweeps past, and Susan grabs the fabric with her good hand. She whispers, "Help me." Hannah stares in disgust. Susan must look rough. Nevertheless, Hannah allows her to cling to her arm, her shoulder, while she straightens. Hannah nearly topples with the crippled weight of her, but finally Susan is as upright as she'll get.

"Time for a walking stick, Mother Susan. Shall I get you the broom?"

"Don't mock me. It'll be you, next."

Hannah shakes off Susan's grip as though she were contagious. She gathers the trail of her long robe and hurries toward Father's warm chamber. Now that his furor is spent, no doubt she will reap the guilty goodness, the crumbs of his remorse. The children head for the latrines—how can anything come out when nothing's gone in?—and Susan is alone.

She shuffles to the bedroom, to blurry rows of grey cots. One night away, and she sees it as though she is a stranger: bad smells, cheap beds. It reminds her of the state-run children's ward where she spent many unhappy nights years ago. A pale shape out of place. The slow swing of it. Susan's hands are on the damp cotton before her eyes adjust. The strange tilt of neck. Hair cut to the scalp. Face, swollen and blue, tongue protruding in ghastly taunt, blood trickling out her nostrils. Rebekah.

"God have mercy."

Susan stumbles and gasps. She wipes her bruised face with her sleeve. She limps back to shut the door. The children must not see. When she hears the familiar lope of Silas's footsteps in the hall, Susan opens a crack and calls: "Cousin Silas, tell Ruth to take the children to the classroom. Get Father Ernst. Now."

"Are you all right?" he says. He pushes, but Susan blocks the door with her body.

"It's urgent." She shuts the door firmly, drags a chair in front, and settles herself on its seat.

She would prefer not to see him just now, Father Ernst. It has been some time since he demonstrated that tenor of rage. Memaw always handled him easily, or so it seemed. He doted on Deborah, too. Mary could sometimes pacify him; she was the most submissive. They likely took turns easing his delicate states, cajoling, distracting him. Stoking his ego like a campfire; tending it, feeding it just so, to keep a steady flame. Not letting it burn out. Not letting it billow and devour the forest beyond.

He used to have other outlets for his temper—challenging politicians in public debate, blasting enemies in his famous sermons, whittling their loud resistance down to mewling and whinging, then nothing. He's lost more than a favourite pastime by coming below. Now there are just women and children. Mayhap he has lost sight of the true opposition. Boys—his own blood, about to become men, his only rivals. Girls—good only to be broken as brides.

Father Ernst's brisk knock wakes Susan, who has drifted off. He tries to open the door and, of course, it bangs against the chair back. She scrapes the chair legs as she moves it aside, and Father Ernst cringes at the noise. He throws the door wide, but will not enter. He says nothing. Does he even see the body?

"I found her just so when I come back from the Sit," says Susan.

She steps closer. She will make him look at his work. All of it. The low-generator lighting is dim, but it cannot hide Susan's swollen eye, her split lip. Icing would have helped, but they've no ice. There'd been no time before the Sit for a cool compress.

Father Ernst's eyes land on her. Flit away.

She watches him squint. Hesitate. His eyes dart to and from the figure hanging in the room beyond her. His throat works. A flash of vulnerability—perhaps fear, perhaps shock? Then nothing. That same smooth face, hard as bunker walls and equally impenetrable. Whatever Father Ernst might feel is locked inside that vault.

"Cut her down," he says. "Take the body to the pantry storage." Then he leaves.

Obviously Susan cannot do it alone. She can hardly stand.

Hardly walk. Silas lurks in the hall shadows. Silas, book smart and almost useless, dry heaves when he enters the room.

"Come now," she says, "show some strength."

The boy wrestles with Rebekah's stiff limbs. She must have been hanging for most of the day. Silas climbs the cot and cuts her down.

The noose is woven from Rebekah's own hair. Susan pulls a fresh bed sheet from storage and spreads it on the floor. "Wrap her good," she says. Silas yanks Rebekah's skirt to reposition her and Susan swats him. "Show some respect."

The boy half-carries, half-drags Rebekah. Susan strips the bed. Soiled sheets. A fusty smell in the blanket. A few curls. Susan twines them together and tucks them in her pocket. Beneath the pillow, Susan finds an infant's baptism bonnet. Always they are white on white, a token of purity given unto God. This abomination in Susan's trembling hand is white cotton embroidered with morbid black thread. It is Rebekah's signature smocking, impeccable and delicate, with what looks like dark seed pearls. On closer inspection, they are tiny bits of repurposed ballpoint pens: finials, caps, nibs, plungers, and circular centre bands, all jet. Black silk ribbon and lace trim, probably from Rebekah's own mourning shawl, to finish. It is chilling, exquisite work. Susan stuffs the bonnet into her dress pocket.

The girl was wrong in the head. Sick.

Susan recalls hearing Rebekah hack and spit, hack and spit, all morning, weeks ago. Nothing to puke up, but still the girl heaved, and her skin was tinged green with nausea. Her despair, the salt traces of tears—so unlike Rebekah. But so very like Susan herself when she was with child, which had been often enough, before.

Susan piles the sheets. The mattress, when she hoists and leans it bare against the wall, reveals another message. It's a poem embroidered by Rebekah's fine hand in multi-coloured thread, all the precious end bits.

Housework

Lard soap slivers
Bob and float
Scrub Scour Rinse
Scrub Scour Rinse

Rag dunk bucket
Wringing wringing
Red knuckled attrition,
My sackcloth and ashes

Stains lift—Hallelu!
Stains set—coffee, semen, so much blood
Never absolved
Verily, verily, upon my weeping knees.

What to make of this heresy? Susan wrestles with the sodden mattress, attempts to flip it so the poem is against the wall, but then the terrible stain faces outward, and she is not certain which is more upsetting. *The poem.* Father Ernst will set to in a fierce rage if he sees it. And yet, something about the terse words speak to her own life. Who has washed more floors than Susan? Scrubbed as many laundry loads? No one. She drapes a clean sheet to cover the soiled bits and, beyond exhausted, collapses on her cot. *Verily, verily.* She hauls her feet up and stretches carefully on her side. She and Rebekah weren't close, but still Susan has been abandoned. Again.

She starts to cry.

She stops. It never helps. She must build resolve; this is no time for cowardice. Instead, Susan mouths the words: *Take me with you.* She cannot speak her furtive prayer aloud.

CHAPTER 23

Father Ernst ejects Hannah from his chamber. As she begins to voice complaint, he raises a menacing hand. She scurries. Father Ernst slams the door and locks it. He paces. He gnaws on his thumb knuckle. This is like his troubling dream: Father Ernst holds a miniature bunker made of glass, like a snow globe from his childhood. He shakes and shakes it. He marvels at the tiny blizzard inside, and then it is slipping from his grasp, falling, smashing on the concrete floor at his feet. Tiny figures writhe, impaled on shards of glass.

How did the Dark Angel infiltrate? Mayhap when Cousin Paul left, days ago. The unsealing: that sudden movement of air, contaminating his domain. Rebekah had been moping about ever since. And now this final disgusting act.

"Female trouble," says Father Ernst aloud. "The spiritual crisis."

Ruth, floundering. Susan, suddenly impertinent, and Hannah unbearable—Satan must have lain in wait and slipped inside their haven unnoticed. Satan sought out the fickle heart of woman to turn it, to rot it in the core.

Unless Satan was already among us.

Father Ernst freezes. The boy. So like his dark-haired traitor sire. Those black eyes always judging, the smirk on his wide lips. Infecting his blond and blue-eyed tribe. Of course! When the boy left to scavenge food, Evil lost its Host. Satan would not ascend; he already owns that domain. Topside is virulent with sin—the whole earth, Hell and Purgatory at once. Only here, below the rubble, here in Father Ernst's Holy nest, persists a light so pure and white that Satan yearns to put it out.

Father Ernst rakes fingers through his hair.

Judas. He should have never allowed the boy entrance. Should have known that serpent's seed would triumph even over his daughter Ruth's goodness. Now, when he should be building strength and growing his tribe to prepare for the glorious Ascension, when he should focus on the Seventh, he will have to roust out demons.

If Paul returns, he must be destroyed. An exorcism, a spiritual cleansing and a culling, all in one ritual. Father Ernst did not expect to fight this battle below. Yet, of course, he must. For the Devil lurks in every heart. Father Ernst has grown complacent, just like the Family. Had he been more vigilant, perhaps he could have saved her.

Rebekah. Deborah's youngest and most elusive child. Coy. Often silent. Something in those watchful eyes rankled him, even when she was a toddler. His second home on the farm, Deborah's, was abundant as opposed to Memaw's clean, quiet A-frame. Noise and mess; children and the chaotic evidence of their lives were everywhere—diapers, crayons, toys strewn about the carpet. Rambunctious Saul and Matthew, his first sons. Then Jeremiah, whom he chose as his Second, and Thomas, also spirited. The boys were devout, mostly obedient. Dead, now. Two martyred in the Standoff, two whilst procuring for the bunkered Family.

The other girl, the eldest, was wilful. Corrupted in her teens. Father Ernst will not utter her name. The first to defy him. Shouting matches, subterfuge. She stopped at nothing to provoke his ire—and that was settled, finally, when he discovered her fornicating with a Mexican field hand she met in town. His bones nourished the pigs. How it broke the mothers' hearts, particularly Deborah's, to strike the girl's name from the Family Bible. To shear her, gather her siren's locks, and burn them with all of her clothes, with all her worldly possessions. Ernst stripped her while the other men held her arms. He spoke in tongues, whipped her in a frenzy. Then she was made to walk through the fire of her former life, naked, away from their bounty, away from their goodness and the sanctity of their land. Weeping. For shame, Lilith!

Father Ernst sits heavily on his bed. He toes the rug beneath his feet. That failure injured him profoundly. Still, it served to instruct. No one who witnessed the casting-out would ever forget it. Rebekah, compared to her sister, was meek. But something was astray. Of all the children, Rebekah with her unruly mop, her pale scrutiny, would appear suddenly at his elbow while he sipped bourbon and wrote sermons and speeches, late into the night. Watching him. Or when he rehearsed at the pulpit in an otherwise empty church. The growing awareness of her relentless gaze would make the hair stand at the back of his neck, gooseflesh rise on his arms.

Once they'd gone to ground, it was different. Rebekah could no longer amble the shadows like a cat. He'd watched her mature slowly. Made his intentions known. Deborah and Memaw protested, said it wasn't natural to take his own child. But who else was there to wed? Out of respect, he waited until they both passed before proceeding.

Rebekah took up her role with a reticence that, frankly, unnerved him. He intended to cure her of that impassivity, as he had the others. But their relations were stilted, repellent. He always had to push. She would lie there, staring, unaccommodating. She didn't fight or argue, but her flesh never yielded. Had to do everything himself. Fumbling with her clothes was the worst. Ernst could not stand those wrathful eyes, judging. He would roll her over, obliterate her face in the pillow, tear at her skirts. He relied on God to fuel him—how else could he perform his conjugal duties?

She'd borne Leah and Abel, the two youngest. But as soon as Hannah ripened, he took her next and henceforth left Rebekah undisturbed. A weakness. Was Ernst himself being punished for not tending Rebekah's due course as wife?

That shall not happen again, he swears.

He checks the lock on his door. Beside the bed is a bookshelf, which he moves away from the wall. Behind it, his hands feel for an indentation. He presses, puts his weight behind it, and a segment of wall gives with a click. The secret door swings open, and Father Ernst steps inside the hidden storage room, shuts the door behind him. Low lighting flickers and hums. Two shelves of bottled water, emergency supplies, cases of dehydrated high-protein meals, military issue. Gun vault and secure panic room behind another hidden bulletproof door on his right. It's dead quiet here, secluded, and dry with dust. A whiff of the forbidden stirs him. He falls on his knees. *Be sober, be vigilant; for your adversary the Devil walks about like a roaring lion, seeking who he may devour.*

He raises his hands. "Forgive me, Father in Heaven." Father Ernst removes his robe, folds it, and sets it on the floor beside him. Same with the flannel shirt he wears beneath. He unbuckles his belt and rolls it in one hand. He repeats a mantra: "He who is in you is greater than he who is in the world."

Belt in hand, he begins the mortification of his own flesh, thumping his shoulders, his back. Leather on skin builds heat. The hits land hard, slapping and stinging. It builds to an exquisite song of pain and pleasure, an adrenal rush, purification tearing away the faults and frailties of this human body, this mind. Leading him at last to redemption, to the Eternal Garden, to a purity of thought, word, and deed. The flesh flayed and beaten. The heart baked like a coal and eaten.

CHAPTER 24

Paul lies trussed in the dirt, the taste of blood in his mouth. Rope binds his ankles and wrists, tied tightly with a short length between. Everything hurts, especially his head, which feels like it was struck with a rock. More, it's humiliating. He's completely helpless, and it's all his fault. An unforgiveable lapse in vigilance.

He can hear the scuffle of feet in the undergrowth, but from this angle he can't see his attacker. From the glimpse earlier: slight build, similar height to him, but stronger. Very good with a rope. Darker skin, dressed in forest colours—bark and cone and leafy green—two black braids. Not one word out of him, despite Paul's attempts to talk. Maybe he doesn't speak English.

"*Por favor*," he tries again, the way his mother taught him. He licks his lips. "*Dejarme tranquilo.*"

A snicker.

Paul strains his ears toward the sound. "Speak Spanish? *Habla española?*"

"Your Spanish is pretty bad."

He hadn't spoken it in years. Not since the Family stopped selling produce in local county markets in order to prepare for the Great Standoff. Memaw and the women had made friends with many farmers and field workers, and all of the children had played together.

"But at least you know some."

The voiçe is softer than he expected. Female?

"Who are you? What do you want? I got nothing," says Paul.

"Lie. You've got a knife, canteen, waterproof matches. Oh yes, and a nice rifle." The click and release of the magazine, the roll of cartridges in the case as they are counted. "Fully loaded. All mine now. Let's see what else."

Hands unzip Paul's coveralls. Pat him down. "Coke can? Where'd you get this?" The hunter tosses it to the ground—obviously doesn't know it can be used to start a fire. Paul might know more about survival in the wild, and that could be useful. Hands reach inside his coveralls, smoothing the length of his chest and belly, down to his genitals, which they squeeze, and around to his buttocks. "Not much meat. You're a bony one." Again, a chuckle.

Paul shivers. Could this hunter want to defile him? Or roast him, feast on his malnourished limbs?

"Thought that rattler was going to get you." The hunter crouches over him and holds his face between both hands. They stare at one another. "You move fast."

Paul has never seen such eyes—darker than Ruth's, darker even than his father's, a deep velvety brown with the blackest centres. Colours so rich he could fall into them, obliterated. He—a miniaturized white figment—reflected back. The face is composed, symmetrical, with strong brows, high cheekbones, full lips. Skin clear and smooth, a beautiful brown. Not male, but not particularly feminine. "Are you a girl?" he whispers.

"I'm a woman," she says, and knees him in the gut.

Paul groans. He should have known better.

"Where are your people? Talk."

"I'm alone," says Paul. "Promise."

"In the forest, yes. I was watching. Before that. Where d'you come from?"

"Across the sands."

"Where you been living? You're so white you'd scare a maggot."

Paul says nothing.

"Who are you with? What side are you on?"

Paul is dazed. He says, "I'm on God's side."

"God," she says. "What does that even mean anymore?" She sighs. Leans back, shifting her weight, crushing him, and he stifles a cry.

"Sorry," she says, and then she is off of him, holding the Ruger, towering above, as though considering her next move. She cocks her head to one side.

"Please let me go," he says. "I'm no threat to you."

"Obviously." She smiles. "But maybe you've got friends nearby. Maybe you're scouting ahead. If I let you go now, it could be me tied up and left to die."

"It's not like that," he says.

She lifts the rifle and squints down the site, raises it as though aiming at the sun, then swings it back to point at his forehead.

"Forgive me my sins and trespasses," he whispers. "Prepare me for the final journey. May I rest with Your love in the Garden forever."

"Okay, that's enough out of you, God Boy," she says. She lowers the rifle and slings it over a shoulder. Unties the short rope connecting his wrists and ankles and pulls it, forcing him to his feet. She loops the rope around his neck as though he's a dog on a leash. "We're moving out," she says.

Paul stumbles through bush and branch and vine, hands tied. He moves his wrists up and down as quickly as possible while rotating them in half circles. It'll take time, but this will loosen the ropes. On the Farm, children used to have to compete to see who'd break free from bondage first. Young Thomas had set an impressive record, escaping the trunk of Father Ernst's locked car in under two minutes, while a weeping Silas had to be rescued time and again. Paul did okay but loathed being trapped in confined spaces.

Paul is forced to walk quickly, and without his arms free he loses balance. She yanks if he is too slow, if he misses a cue about veering left or right around trees, and hisses when he makes too much noise, floundering in dry leaves or cracking dead branches underfoot. Twice she stops, listening to the forest like an animal. A fox, Paul thinks. She has the small-footed grace of one, the cunning resourcefulness, too. His breath comes ragged. He can't help it—he's weak and tires easily. This annoys her when she is listening to the trees, the earth, and she covers his mouth with a hand, quieting him. Her fingers are warm, small, and calloused. They smell of pine and topsoil. Paul considers biting, but he knows this will only beget more violence.

"Where are we going?" he asks again.

She makes a chirping sound, repeats it, then releases a mournful call from deep in her throat, one that raises gooseflesh on his skin.

She waits, calls again. An answering trill, not far away. She's bringing him to her people. He'll have even less chance to escape. There is space between his wrists now, almost enough to slip a hand out.

"You've got my stuff. Let me go!" He resists the tether when she pulls.

"If you were really alone, you'd be glad for the company," she says.

"Please!"

"Kneel," she says.

But Paul is not listening. He's circling, panicked. Movements, sly and sure, in the treetops and down among the gnarled roots, behind piled leaves and dripping vines. Eyes fall upon him. He works one wrist free, then the other. Tears at the rope around his neck. The huntress sweeps his feet out from under him with the rifle and, tied or not tied, Paul crashes to the ground.

CHAPTER 25

Rebekah's naked body is laid out on the pantry counter, neck bruised and broken, her shorn head at an odd angle. Blood at her nostrils. Tongue stiff, protruding. Ruth tries to look away. She is to help, a first.

Susan, draped in the rubber apron, holds the carving knife, the cleaver. She explains how it will go. She worked in a meat processing plant as a teen. Later, she butchered cattle, sheep, and goats on the Farm. "Not too different," she says. "Repulsive but unavoidable." Hours of grisly work ahead of them. "You been sheltered 'til now," she says, "but no more."

"Can't we take her topside?" whispers Ruth. "Bury her in the orchard. The sands?"

"Father's orders."

"Then why don't *he* do it?"

Susan hands her a deboning knife, sinister and curved, longer than the one Ruth keeps at her belt. This is really happening. Rebekah's body is violet and cold. When she touches it, it feels like thick rubber, like the hot water bottle, the latrine plungers. Not at all like skin. The small meat of her breasts falls to each side. Nipples are darker, puckering. Slight rounding in the belly. Wiry hair between her thighs. Ribs and hips and all the delicate bird bones of her wrists, shoulders, collar.

An urgent thrum whispers: run, run! Hysteria bubbles up, and a trembling overtakes her. "Mother Susan, I can't," she says. She drops the knife. Gags.

Susan slaps her, to no avail.

"No, no." Ruth collapses on the floor.

"Get up or get out!" Susan's foot prods her. Pity? Or total exasperation? Either way, Ruth scuttles to the Great Hall, wiping her face on her sleeves. She slinks to her bed and weeps until, exhausted, she drops into a confused sleep.

It feels like mere minutes later she is being shaken. Mother Susan is at her bedside shouting, "Wake up."

"Already?"

"Father Ernst called us."

"Now?" Ruth blinks. There's a battering, a breach inside her head.

"Get the others."

Ruth falls back to the pillow. Her temples throb. She is fogged by a terrible dream that stokes her grief and horror: Rebekah's nude corpse shuffling toward her in the long exit tunnel. Ruth could not escape—the Mission Pole and ladder were gone, just the inner blast door bolted above her, out of reach. Backed into the farthest corner, she had to look upon Rebekah's broken face advancing. Rebekah raised her arms and moaned. The surprise—she did not strike, only held her arms aloft for a final embrace.

Ruth says, "Think he's calling the Ascension?"

"Not for you or me to say." There's a wildness about Susan. Clearly, she has not slept, and she has not cleaned herself. The stain on her long skirt—blood and gore.

Ruth licks her lips. She tries again. "If we don't go now, we won't be able to. It's hard to climb the ladder."

Susan says, "Get up."

"The children will need help. Carrying."

"Enough!"

Ruth hugs her knees to her chest. She tucks her feet under the hem of the nightdress. Susan is frozen, glaring. Her cheek is a ripe plum, soft and purple, in the otherwise gaunt face above her cadaverous body. Tension surges like a static charge, the promise of violence.

Ruth owes her something. What? She swings her legs off the mattress and lowers her feet. Steadies her breath. Pounding in her ears. "Shall I stitch the sacred pouch? For the cairn?" Ruth's blood rags are hidden there.

"No pouch for the unnamed. No burial. Father Ernst instructs us to Martyr and none other. This was the Devil's work."

"Oh." A ragged noise comes from her horrified mouth. Poor Rebekah: outcast, orphaned in the afterlife, locked out of God's Garden. Gentle Rebekah, alone, pressed to the wrong side of His gate for eternity.

Then relief, too, curdled by guilt: Ruth's secret will stay safe.

"Both of you, shut up." Hannah huddles in the bedclothes in her own cot for a change.

"He didn't send for you?" Susan asks Hannah.

"He has a lot on his mind. But your wicked words will make their way to his ear."

"Please, no," says Ruth.

Susan, brave or indifferent or savage from her night of labour, tears the top quilt from Hannah's bed. "Time you did something useful," she says. "Sort her things. Find something to burn." Susan leaves—to wash, Ruth hopes.

At Rebekah's bare cot, Ruth squats and pulls the trunk out from underneath. She unclasps the latch and lifts the wide lid. Rebekah's scent. All her belongings. Not hers, actually. She outgrew everything since coming to ground. She was only a child of eleven, then. These are hand-me-downs from previous mothers.

Hannah, hovering, says, "You can handle this," and leaves in a huff.

Ruth picks up the new quilt. The edges have a crisp finish, but when she flips a corner, she sees that the backing layer is an old bed sheet, worn thin and stained, a map of those earthly elements the body cannot contain. Strange choice for Rebekah, who prided herself on creating pretty, reversible patterns. No one has seen it yet. Ruth can't bear to look, either. It's as though Rebekah is still here, folded up with these coveted cloth squares. She sets it aside. Four dresses and slips, which she piles on the mattress. Three flannel nightshirts. Underthings, also inherited. Woollen stockings, patched and darned and almost worn through again. Sweaters: those can be unravelled and reknit or simply worn large, layered. Baby clothes that Rebekah stitched and embroidered. Her handiwork.

At the bottom in the trunk's far corner, Ruth discovers a small packet. Inside, a beautiful jade comb. She traces it with her finger—flowers on a vine dripping with leaves. This comb sat in the centre of her dad's dresser, just out of reach. "Off limits," he said. It belonged to her mother. Why is it in Rebekah's trunk? Ruth presses it to her nose—dust and the barest hint of lavender from the sachets they tucked in with their clothes. Inside the packet are faint pencil scratchings, words and more words, when she carefully unfolds and flattens it on her lap. A diary? A letter?

Susan returns in a fresh set of clothes. "Well?"

Ruth hides the comb and its wrapping between her thighs. She has nothing for the burn pile. She tosses a slip. "Her scent is all over it."

Susan nods and takes the bundle when she leaves.

In the Great Hall, Father Ernst's pulpit has been wheeled out and the benches set one behind another. A pall lingers like sickness in the warmed room: singed hair, burning gristle, charred bone. Wafts of roast every time Susan opens the oven door.

More sermon than funeral. That's how Ruth remembers the Unnaming Ceremony for her father. It was held during the first heady days of bunkering, when her father's absence felt theoretical still.

At Father's bidding, Silas climbs off the squeaking stationary bike. Soon there will be lard to grease it.

"Places, everyone," he says.

Hannah takes her Vestal Cushion to the front. Ruth and the children fit on one bench. Their lost tribe fills the others: Memaw, Deborah, Mary, Deborah's teen boys, all the sickly infants, the countless stillborns. Ruth sees them, plain as Silas standing in front.

Rebekah and her gruesome rope hold court in the centre. No Paul, which is a relief. But none of the Standoff Martyrs are there and not her traitor father, either. She blinks and the images dissipate, leaving friendless wooden benches in their wake.

Susan sinks her ladle in the pail, and it clangs against the side. Ruth can hear the water sloshing. Her tongue is as dry as an old shoe. Each child gets a mouthful. Susan comes to her last. Fills the ladle right up and nods. "Go on." It's more than her share, but Ruth can't stop once she tastes it. One, two swallows. She holds the last bit in her mouth as long as she can.

Leah crawls onto Ruth's lap. She wants a hug, a kiss. Ruth lets the last of her water fall into the girl's surprised mouth. Should have never identified the poor thing's birth mother. Now look. Ruth opens her shawl to let her in.

Father Ernst strides to the pulpit, brisk, full of purpose. He grips the lectern, and his mouth moves imperceptibly as he scans the room. Could be he's counting heads. His voice booms. "Sin is a fire that catches all kindling. Now, one among us is gone."

"Her name is lost forever," they say.

Ruth squeezes Leah.

"Yea, that darkness swallows the light. Yet we do not hide in fear. We walk the perilous night armed with the truth, with the Doctrine, and with God's light in our hearts. We offer ourselves up to fight in God's Great Army. Amen."

"Amen."

Father looks at the vent guard in the ceiling. He cocks his head, like he's listening. He says, "Samson fought the Philistines and knowingly sacrificed himself to smite the enemy. This most Holy martyr we embrace."

"Holy Martyrs, most blessed sacrifice," they say.

"Just so, we sent our soldiers to battle. They released the Burning Light. Staged a war on wicked America in the Great Standoff."

"Holy Martyrs, who wait for us now in God's Garden," they say.

"Judas Iscariot, traitor, betrayed God's only Son."

"Enemy of God, we fight thee," they say.

Leah buries her cries in Ruth's wet neck.

Father Ernst continues. "Later, filled with remorse, Judas hung himself. Laid his life to waste. But him we do not embrace. For the sinner's cowardice ended in self-murder. There is no rest or redemption for him. God, in his wisdom, did not grant him peace. Father of Life."

They say, "Your will be done on earth as in Heaven."

"Lord of Life," intones Father Ernst.

"Hear our prayers," they reply.

"Just so, this Cousin took her life, that which is God's and mine alone. She shall rove the pestilent earth, the polluted seas, for eternity. She shall pace outside the gate of God's Holy Garden and shall never enter, and she shall never find rest. In our hour of need, she forsook God and the Family and there is no forgiveness for her. Your kingdom come."

"Your will be done. Amen."

Words echo and ring. Ruth stands to respond, sits to listen, just like the others. Stands. Sits. She is stupefied. How will she explain this to Paul? He knew something was wrong. Why else bid her check on Rebekah? That uncanny silence, her despair. The urgent message she spelled on Ruth's hand: *guilt*, or was it *quilt*? All for what? One final act, terrifying and irrevocable. Ruth is not ashamed for Rebekah, as Father is. She is ashamed that she, that none of them, helped her. Her teeth grind. Heat runs in her veins. This is anger. Ruth is beginning to feel dangerous.

After the ceremony, Mother Susan and Hannah carry trays to table. Grey water porridge with an oily heft in each bowl. On Father's invitation, Silas commences. Then Hannah. The children grab utensils. Father Ernst savours each spoonful, eyes closed, moustache trembling as his mouth slowly works. Ruth watches, horrified. She will not join them. She grips her skirt under the table. She wants to scream, to kick.

Susan leans in the kitchen alcove. She says, "Go slow, children. Bellies been empty a while."

"Join us, Mother Susan." Father Ernst beckons her toward the girls' bench.

She stares.

"Sit," he says. "I insist."

Susan limps over but cannot lift her leg high enough to straddle the bench. Rather than move over, Hannah sidles out to let her in. Susan lowers stiffly beside Ruth, hands folded on the table in front of her. No bowl. Hannah reclaims her spot at Father's left hand.

Ruth has eaten nothing in days. Water helps, but she's had

precious little. She knows she can go almost three weeks without food as long as she has water. She spoons the gruel, raises the spoon. Susan's eyes bore into hers and that brooding heaviness quells the pang in her middle. She lowers the spoon. Susan bows onto clasped hands, her lips move in silent prayer. Her eyes close. Ruth lifts the spoon again. She looks from Susan's profile to her bowl, back again. Hunger wins. Metal on tongue waters her mouth. Warm broth, the sweet and salt of it. Thick chew of meat. She grinds it in the back molars into a paste that she swallows. The greasy after-coat is a ghost glaze, indicting her.

CHAPTER 26

The children are pink-cheeked from meat. The twins play a hand-clapping game that Susan hasn't heard in months. The boys want more, but she refuses. It's happened before—shrunken bellies rejecting second servings. Nothing worse than puking and, frantic, trying to eat the sick off their own shoes. As far as Susan can tell, they're oblivious; they haven't connected this food to where it came from. Or else they cannot bear the truth. How can it not alter them in some primal way? She observes them as though from a faraway planet, through the cold lens of space, remote as the moon.

She stands inside the kitchen alcove, scrubbing the roast pans. What a grisly, crackling mess. From here she can lean and take in the Great Hall, the children, Silas working the generator, and Father Ernst's locked door. He's inside again. Who knows what madness will overtake him next? Susan has not uttered a word, but fear consumes her. Like the tropical snake she saw in a television documentary as a child—fear has an unhinged jaw, it can swallow anything.

Her mind cannot settle. Memaw. The Farm. Rebekah's face, Rebekah's limbs, pools of sticky blood. Susan's stepfather, his figure and voice only, the face lost to her, finally, after so many years. Now and again it is Father Ernst's face on that other cruel body. She shakes herself. *Focus.*

Ruth is right: They will need strength to climb the ladder if they are to ever leave this place. The children will need help. Silas and Ruth have some wits about them, at least. Father Ernst is more intent than ever on burrowing inside his mystifying dreams. The Ascension is clearly no longer a priority. His plans for the bunker are vague but seem to hinge on Ruth transforming into a graceful matriarch, somehow embodying the spirits of the two other Ruths: Memaw and their only daughter, who died giving birth.

"I'll eat my own hand first," Susan mutters.

From the tunnel door, Ruth slips into the Great Hall and heads to the kitchen. She sets her hunting sack on the counter and cleans off her beloved knife. "For you," the girl says, shuffling her feet. "Need your strength."

Susan lifts the bag and weighs it in her hands. A half-pounder. The girl noticed she would not eat the other flesh. The girl cared. Emotion heats Susan's throat and she coughs to distract from that ambush, tenderness. "Thank you," she says, and shoos Ruth away. She skins the rodent quickly, guts it, and places the still-warm body in the oven to cook.

"What's the difference," she says aloud. It's all skin and muscle and organs and indigestibles. Couldn't rats also grieve? Are they equally horrified to find themselves, from time to time, desperately feeding on one of their own?

"A matter of survival," Father Ernst said. "Aught we know, civilization depends on *us*; extinction's far worse than slitting Martyred skin, hanging it to drain, divvying meat in the kitchen."

But how can God condone it?

On the Farm they often ate meat, especially the men. But

Memaw declined, ate only grains, vegetables, fruits, and eggs. *Of these ye shall freely eat.* That was her motto. The days that Father Ernst led a haltered animal to the culling stone floor in the small, windowless hut at the edge of the field, he sought refuge with one of the other wives. He delivered the blow, slit the throat, or fired the gun. He bade Susan do the rest.

Lately, the entire bunker has called to her mind that kill house, with its stagnant air, bloodied and fecal, animal terror and hopelessness pumped into the cold stink. Sometimes she can still feel their struggle—rolling eyes and bucking hooves—the snorting and screaming. Then surrender, which sometimes felt like a blessing. Their deaths left her weak with a private sorrow she never discussed with anyone. Of them all, Susan can set her mind to any task and plod through, regardless of inner turmoil. Regardless of her own vicarious suffering. She learned to do that early in that terrible house of violence in the place she was born and from which she eventually fled.

So much is a circle coming back around. All that she abandoned chases her of late. Hunger and terror and hurting—the accompanying isolation, the paranoia.

It can't go on.

Susan is bone-tired when she finally makes her way to the girls' bedroom. Voices inside. Thought they'd be asleep. But there are the chirping twins and breathy Leah. Susan pauses to listen.

"What will we eat in Heaven?" says Rachel.

"Yes, what," says Leah.

Ruth's dreamy voice says, "Peach cobbler. With vanilla ice-cream."

"What's that?"

"Ooh, ice-cream is the best. It's cold and sweet and melts in your mouth. And the cobbler is hot from the oven. It is fruit with jammy sauce and oatmeal on top."

"Oats. Yuck."

"Not like oats we eat here," says Ruth. "You'll love it."

"I can't wait to go to Heaven."

"Me either."

"Soon, maybe."

"Soon."

"Glory, Hallelujah."

Susan clasps her hands and presses them to her lips. Why didn't she think of this sooner? She could deliver the girls from this miserable struggle. Send them swiftly to God's Garden, where they can play and dream and, finally, eat in peace. She herself will suffer—there will be no redemption for her. But she can set the children free. Like so much else in life, this fermenting idea is terrible. Almost impossible to hold in the face of God. But Susan is strong. This is simply one more twisted test that she must pass.

Tonight she will sleep. Tomorrow, her new work begins.

CHAPTER 27

The girls are down. Susan, too, snores fitfully. She was exhausted, the poor woman. More haggard than ever. But Ruth lies awake in bed, cold and preyed upon. Rebekah's absence looms as though her body, which once housed mystery, released it into the air when she died, filling the women's chamber with a secret unrest. The writing—Ruth carefully reaches beneath her mattress, where she hid the comb and its paper wrapping. She lights a candle stub, sets it on the top of her trunk, and holds the page as close as she dares without singeing it. This is Rebekah's hand, certainly—ghostly loops, precise crosses, and dots—her fading cursive.

Girlhood

Morning
Set to chores, sweeping and scrubbing
I am bored
Pinning up sheets in the dirt yard
Men's clothes, sweat-stained, reeking tobacco, manure,
gasoline—I scrub, scrub on the lawn
Lunch bell
Pitch the water
Soup and Memaw's bread with hard cheese and lemonade
When no one's looking, take one more slice

Afternoon
Legs pumping, I outrace the boys
I am strong
This field, this orchard, my Empire
I climb the sap-sticky bark of a tree; nest in leafy branch
No one can see me, not even God
Dinner bell
Climb higher
Calling and calling my name but no one comes looking
I laugh and laugh

Twilight
Itchy backside, my stomach sings
I am hungry
Supper was yams with salted chives
Maybe wild greens, cob corn, and sliced radish; maybe tomato,
sweet as a grape pulled from the vine
Vespers
I'm forsaken
Legs cramp and mosquitoes bite and I've got to pee
I won't leave; still, nobody comes

Nightfall
Bats skitter, owl hoots from her perch
I am tired

Lift cotton skirt, hug the gnarled trunk
Don't need them in Heaven so toss stockings and bloomers to
the grass below, piss in the wind
Midnight
So sleepy
Coyote carries my underpants off in his mouth
Moon spills silver on my face and limbs

She sees me
Knows where to look

Ruth reads it again and again. It could be her up on that tree branch, hiding. She remembers doing the same thing when they lived aboveground, when the children were allowed to play freely until dark. Why doesn't the girl climb down for dinner? But somehow Ruth understands. She can't put it into words, not like Rebekah has done. But something flutters inside when Ruth reads the poem and when those pictures enliven her own small mind. Giving up comforts for freedom is something the Family can relate to. But this is some other kind of freedom entirely, the one Rebekah sat waiting for. Freedom from the Family itself, gifted by the moon.

Silas described the hanging to her in far more detail than she'd wanted, and this haunts her. It took conviction and physical strength, what Rebekah did. Severing her hair, tying a noose. Fixing it high in the ceiling and climbing onto the bed's foot rails. Why? At least her earthly pains are over. Now begins the endless turmoil of God's fierce punishment.

"Forgive her, Father. Show Your mercy. Let her wandering soul rest in Your Garden, I beg You. Amen."

Ruth is sick with guilt. The anger that churned inside now feeds on itself. Her mind jumps from fresh wounds to older, festering ones. "The Mothers keep dying," she said to Paul years back. And he said, "Yes. Do you ever wonder about the men? There used to be a church full of them."

Ruth remembers packing, the church divided into sections: bedding, dry and canned goods, tools and weapons. Personal items were grouped by family name. Women canned preserves in great batches. Older kids helped. Men carried heavy loads to the bunker door, stacking them outside. Only Father Ernst and the builder actually entered. For Ruth and the other little children it was a time of great excitement—singing, praying, and speaking in tongues. A recklessness infused their play as they careened around skids piled high above their heads.

Paul prodded her. "Think, Ruth. Why did no one else come below?"

Ruth said, "They were Martyred in the Burning Light, of course. Soldiers who fought in God's army."

Paul slowly shook his head, and she knew she'd said the wrong thing. She was missing his point, as usual. Truthfully, Ruth had expected their dad to join them below. Expected all the families to be there, not just Father Ernst's wives and offspring. She and Paul were the only exceptions. Their dad's betrayal was devastating to

Ruth. How could he, with poor Father Ernst declared an enemy of the state and government sharp-shooters surrounding the compound to pick off Martyrs one by one? And how could she love a traitor?

Paul's questions gnawed at her, so much so she even approached Father Ernst. The blue-green of his eyes rushed like river water. "Did Cousin Paul put that in your head?" he boomed. "Men always come to blows. One bull per herd. I alone am Adam, God's first Son. Remember that."

Boys disappeared the closer they got to manhood. "No coincidence," Paul muttered once. Ruth pinched to shut him up. Still he whispered, "How many babies were stolen in the night? It's not Satan's work, it's Father's will." How could he say such a thing? If Paul is cast out, Ruth will be alone in this world. Bereft. Life will be as it is now—empty, pointless, her relentless fears and half-thoughts stuttering into madness. No one to talk to. No one left to trust.

Unless.

They'd been bunkered for about a month when Silas made a dolly with corn silk hair and grass skirt for himself and Ruth to play with. He was whipped and locked up. Wailing filled the bunker and Ruth cringed, willing him to silence. Even as a child he was slow and desperate for affection. He could not grasp Father Ernst's new rules separating boys from girls—he and Ruth had crawled the same linoleum squares in Mary's topside kitchen with impunity while her dad worked the field. It was as if he could only learn through error, over and over again. They've grown apart, she and Silas, but he still has affection for her.

Ruth gets out of bed. She adds another warm layer and tiptoes down the hall. She has never entered the boys' chamber at night. She checks the hallway twice before sliding open their door. It's smelly, worse than the women's, certainly. Most of the bunks are empty. Abel's hosts a small lump. The cousin bed in the far corner belongs to Silas. What if he resists? Silas might drag her straight to Father Ernst for another whipping, or worse.

Ruth peers as close as she can, her face an inch from the sleeping boy. She shakes him gently at first, then vigorously.

"Cousin!" he says.

She claps a hand over his mouth. "Come," she whispers. She tugs his pyjama sleeve, pulls back the blankets. His eyes widen. She creeps to the door, slips out to wait in the dark. She prays he will hold off complaint long enough to listen and to do what she bids. She has a bold plan coming now—to force the Ascension—and she will need his help. Hannah is a lost cause, and Susan is almost as terrifying as Father Ernst. There is no one else to ask. Besides, who else knows the intricate details of the Doctrine? Who else might know the mysterious signs and symbols that Father Ernst waits on? Mayhap between the two of them they can create some false evidence and convince Father Ernst. She shivers. Such deceit. And yet, why hadn't she thought of this ages ago?

Minutes pass. Finally, Silas appears. He has wet and combed his hair, parting ridiculous bangs in the middle like a gap tooth. Silas reaches for the chest of her thin nightdress. She slaps him, once, across the face. "Philistine!" she whispers. Silas's heat must come strong if his gelding and this foul air cannot dampen desire. "I'll tell Father!"

"Please don't," he whimpers.

"You are not to look at nor touch us, not even the hem of our garments."

"Then why'd you wake me?"

"To talk. Why else?"

"Rebekah used to come for Paul. Weren't for talking."

Ruth is glad the darkness hides her shock. "Liar."

"Am not. I seen them. Thought you knew."

Nothing comes from Ruth's open mouth. The floor tilts. She steadies herself by leaning on the wall behind her. Rebekah and Paul? Impossible!

"I never meant harm. Forgive me, Cousin," he says.

Ruth's jaw snaps shut. A hundred tiny clues rush at once—Rebekah squeezing Paul's fingers in the infirmary, the tender way she cleaned his wounds. That flower—not meant for Ruth, after all. Paul's eyes locking onto Rebekah's. All the things they were saying in some private, silent tongue.

Ruth knows in her belly it is true. She has been a fool, pretending a claim on Paul when, really, she was only their cover—a decoy, lending them excuses for proximity. Ruth will never homestead with him. That image—flowers in her bridal veil—is a falsehood. Did they laugh at her childish fantasy? One tear burns down her cheek. Rebekah is dead, and Paul may as well be.

"Please," Silas begs.

Ruth could use Silas's fear. Make him swear to do her bidding. She wipes her face with a sleeve, grinds down on her molars. Bullying. That's how things get done. She'd be no better and no worse than the rest of them for it.

Suddenly Ruth sees something, a movement behind Silas. It is Rebekah in the dim hallway, hair braided as it once was, wearing a loose robe. An apparition? Her skin glows with a radiant light, and her feet do not touch the cold floor, but hover just above.

"Do you see that?" she whispers.

Silas turns, shakes his head. A hallucination. It happens. Or could this be a vision from God?

Rebekah raises her hands, palms up, reaching slowly to the ceiling. Her chin tilts, her face peers skyward.

Ruth feels those blackened eyes roll onto her and is chastened to the marrow. It's as though Rebekah knows Ruth's dark heart, her hurt and anger. Had she come to punish Ruth for not helping her in time? Or to clean and suture this fresh wound, her and Paul's deception?

"The Ascension," says Ruth. "She's telling us to leave."

"Shh," says Silas, trying to comfort—not touching her shoulder, not touching any part of the startled girl. "It's okay," he says. "I'm here."

There is no one else now, just Silas and Ruth shivering in the frigid hall. A dripping pipe. Quick thud and stutter inside her chest. Confusion. And the sorrowful sounds filling the black night belong to Ruth alone.

CHAPTER 28

Heathens. Bandits. That's who approaches. Wild things in strange clothing with coiled hair. Two armed men step from the greenery. They look similar, but as Paul slows his breath and looks carefully, one to the other, he notices details, differences.

The larger man comes forward, knife unsheathed in hand. He's got Paul's food pack, the one strung in a tree for safe-keeping. That and the gas mask, the UV hood. He didn't notice or didn't bring the throwing stick. He's much taller than Paul, older, and easily twice his weight, with long black hair, and a broad face. He nudges Paul with his foot. A crossbow and arrows over one shoulder, pistol holstered at his hip. Inked patterns curl up the man's bare skin, swirling into phantoms and ogres on his forearms. One huge bicep hosts a dragon. The mark of the Beast: this must be the leader.

"Followed him in, got his things," the huntress says as she reties Paul's wrists with rope. "He came across the sands alone. Says he's on God's side." The way she says 'God' sounds like a mockery. Somewhere, angels weep.

The other man steps into the circle. He's tan and slim, also well muscled. His hair is loose to the shoulders, a mess of corn silk, some tawny, some light. Like Rebekah's when her braid is picked apart, but shorter. "Atta girl," he says. His voice—haunting and familiar. Paul cringes, but the woman does not kick her companion. Instead she moves closer, smiling, and the man laughs.

Paul blinks.

That laugh. Impossible. "Thomas? Thomas!"

The others stare at their mate. Fingers find triggers; hands pull blades from belted leather sheaths. They all point at Paul.

"It's me, Cousin Paul. Untie me, for God's sake!"

Thomas raises a slow palm. "I do know him," he says, "from the life before."

But Thomas does not rush to release Paul's bonds. He inspects Paul, forces open his mouth, counts teeth, squeezes his shoulders, arms, and chest. "You're a runt. The old man still kicking?"

Paul says, "Father Ernst? Yes."

Thomas nods, and his companions step away, giving them privacy. In a softer voice Thomas says, "They all still down there?"

"Not all." Paul chokes out his words. "We thought you died. We sewed the sacred purse. We mourned."

Thomas is more than alive—he is strong, tan, and lithe. The huntress is back beside him now, arms at her hips, head tilted, eyes following their every move. Thomas smiles at her, shrugs. She blinks. Some kind of language carved from silence. Thomas has joined these forest dwelling heretics. He is one of them now, bewitched by an ungodly apostate.

She touches Paul's arm; he flinches. "Sorry I was so rough," she says.

"Sondra doesn't mess around," says Thomas. He calls to the bigger man, "Diego, let's eat. Drink. Find out what he knows. Might be able to use him."

"We have you. Don't need this Bible thumper."

Thomas shrugs like it doesn't matter. "Paul knows the bunker—

numbers, status. He'll know if the stash was moved. I've been gone three years. A lot can change. Up to you, man." He reaches out to touch Diego's shoulder and they hold some silent dialogue. Thomas's fingers slowly move around to cup the back of Diego's neck, massaging it.

"Okay," says Diego, softening. "We'll see."

Soon they are in a small clearing crouched around a campfire. The woman, Sondra, releases Paul's arms and the rope from around his neck but leaves it coiled nearby—probably to remind Paul he's their prisoner. She kneels down to offer her water canteen. He's so thirsty. Still, he hesitates.

"You don't trust me," she says.

He can see the pulse thrum in her neck, she's so close. Smell the musk from her body. In this light, her irises shine jet. His tiny reflection mocks him again, so useless. She tucks thick braids behind her ears and says, "I guess if my people had been killing your people for centuries I'd be suspicious of a kind offer, too."

What did she mean by that? Paul stammers, "S-Sorry. Thank you." He drinks deeply from the canteen.

"I'm serious," she says. "Sorry about before. Didn't know who you were. Thomas has told us about your, uh, family. I know you've been through a lot."

Those same eyes that bore into him without mercy now regard him with compassion. It's confusing. Heat builds in Paul's throat and he swallows, hard. Who are these marauders? What do they want?

Paul clears his throat. "I guess everyone's been through too much nowadays."

When Sondra stands, he has to tilt his head back to see all of her. She is like a slender tree, rooted and full of vitality. That knot of discomfort—shame, guilt, fear—tightens in his belly. Sondra doesn't owe him anything, that's for certain. The reverse, more likely. Had she lost people in the Burning Light? She strides over and settles herself on a log beside Thomas and Diego. Does she belong to them both? Strangely, they show no interest in her. Rather, they lean together, murmuring, laughing at some private joke.

Thomas refuses to look at Paul. But Paul, stupefied, can't stop staring. Thomas is risen. Thomas, healthy and confident, joking with the infidel. Paul strains to remember Deborah's youngest son—four years older than Paul, so never a close playmate. Had occasional tensions with Father, to be expected. Thomas started quietly training Paul to scavenge before he disappeared. In hindsight, Thomas had probably planned his escape for some time. Paul remembers a quiet boy, cooperative and devout. Nothing like the outlaw he's become.

Paul drinks again from the canteen. Thirst slaked, he scans his surroundings. They have nuts and berries, and Thomas gathered ferns that they steam, along with the rabbit, over the fire. If Thomas's friends live off the land, couldn't Paul and the girls? Plenty of life in this old-growth forest. Birdsong, more scampering in the trees, up and down the thick bark of their trunks. He hears a brook nearby. If he makes a run for it, will the current carry him away? Probably it's not deep enough.

Diego licks rabbit grease from thick fingers. "You stab that with your knife? You trap it or what?"

"Used a throwing stick."

Diego says, "No way!"

"Throw hard. Aim for the head." Paul swallows, remembering the hare's final seizure: the body trembling and then the eyes losing light. The stillness. After that, the intermittent hiss of air releasing from the cooling body.

Thomas says, "He always was a good shot as a kid. Make one helluva sniper!"

The group freezes to silence. Paul looks from one to the next.

Thomas says, "Oops. That's awkward."

Sondra says, "Maybe it's time we talk this out." She gestures for Paul to come sit beside her, and the men make room.

The fire's heat soothes his sore limbs, and when Paul looks around the circle, flames lick golden on their faces, softening them. Thomas and Diego lean close on the other side, whispering. Is Diego's arm around Thomas' shoulder? They must be good friends. Paul had never shared a fire with anyone but his father and with Memaw and the other kids. He feels surprisingly calm with these strangers, considering.

Diego says, "You've been buried down in that hole of yours a long time. What, five years?"

"Seven," say Paul and Thomas at once. *Our great tribulation.*

"You might not know," Diego says, "but the American South is pretty much one big war zone. Your *pendejo* leader dropped his dirty bombs and went into hiding. Lots of people died."

"Thousands," says Paul, nodding. This brutal truth sits inside, devouring him.

"People call it the Redneck Rebellion, what started it all. Some folks actually think he's a hero." Diego struggles to keep his voice calm. "At first there was a lot of chaos. Military everywhere. Called the overseas troops home to help sort it out. We built community coalitions to keep the peace in most of the major cities. It worked for a while, believe it or not."

"It still could," says Sondra. "Better than the previous system of governance."

Diego nods. Is he deferring to Sondra? Does that make *her* the leader? Paul reels with all this new information. There had been whispers of a rebel coalition. Thomas had been the first to report it years ago, back when he was still the Family provider.

Sondra continues. "Except right-wing senators released white power prisoners, armed them, made them security militias in the southern states. Called them volunteers, but they're all on payroll. Scary stuff. We've got one hell of a civil war raging. It's why I took those precautions with you."

Paul watches Thomas's face for any reaction. Nothing.

"You're lucky she didn't kill you on sight." Diego says.

"Why'd you come here?" Thomas asks.

"I'm Provider now. Came for food. And the well's tapped out, we need water." Should he say how badly off the Family is? Or would they kill him right now, thinking they don't need him?

"You had meat in your pack."

"Not enough."

"Well, it's gone now. How much water were you gonna carry back over the sands?" Thomas squints at Paul. "You came for something else. What?"

Paul bites his lip. "Wanted to check the woods, make a shelter. Thought to bring them up when I return."

Thomas says, "All of them?"

Paul shakes his head. "Any who'll come but Father. Was going to leave him down."

"Leave him down or put him down?" Thomas, who used to be serious and watchful, lets out another easy laugh. "You rebel!"

"Have you been in the forest all along?" Paul asks. Could he have been so close, all these years?

"No, we were in Atlanta for a while. We travel around, you know. Came back special." Thomas and Sondra and Diego exchange looks. They are like cats, silent and secretive, tuned in to frequencies Paul can't fathom.

"Why did you leave us, Thomas?" Paul tries to keep his voice neutral, but it's hard.

"Why did you stay?" If Thomas feels any guilt, it's buried beneath his skin; no sign of it shows.

"For Ruth. Rebekah. The children." Paul grinds his teeth. "Help me get them out. You've got to."

"Slow down," says Diego. "We've got our own plans."

Sondra says, "People need to pick a side in this fight. You and yours especially, Paul. This is America's ugly past rising up."

"Some would say his people already picked a side," says Diego.

"The kids never had a choice," says Thomas softly.

"We will give them one." That's Sondra, and her words sound final.

Paul's mind churns with all this talk. "What do you want from me?"

Diego says, "Your guns. Thomas says there's a serious stash in that bunker, and we need it. If Ernst is still alive, we're taking him."

"You're not," says Paul.

"Try me. Your white Father started this war and as much as I'd like to end him myself, he'll be tried in an international court."

Sondra gets up and steps into the shadows. The men follow. Paul can't see beyond the bright ring illuminated by campfire, but he hears whispers, voices layering in earnest discussion. Will they kill him now, with a full belly? Or will he be marched across the sands and forced to betray the putrid bunker? Honestly, he couldn't care less about the hidden guns. They can have them.

Bodies, now moving with purpose. Bending, straightening. Laying down bedrolls and putting away their other supplies. They've come to some kind of decision.

Thomas returns to crouch in front of Paul. "Now is the time to tell me if you're gonna be a problem. We're taking Fath—Ernst." Thomas stutters on the name. "Don't be a hero, Paul. You have no idea how big this is."

Paul shakes his head. "I won't, but you can't take anyone else."

"If they cooperate, no one will get hurt."

Paul says, "They're pretty bad off. Might not even make it out."

"We've got a truck waiting. We could take them to medical. I'll see." Thomas shakes his head. "Can't believe they're still there. What the hell have you been eating?" Thomas stares beyond Paul like he's seeing things, the past maybe, and his face contorts.

"You don't want to know, Cousin," says Paul. "Trust me."

CHAPTER 29

Father Ernst paces the length of his chamber. The Ascension taunts him, always out of reach. Over the years he has, perhaps, put too much emphasis on this distant goal. The mothers and children, now even Susan, push with an urgency he resents. They are so literal. To them it is simply about climbing a ladder and opening a door. He tries to explain—there are steps, rules leading to this mythic, cataclysmic release. Each foul mistake drags them back to square one, pushing the likelihood of an actual Ascension farther into the realm of fantasy. He is on a precipice, clawing; a sheer drop lures him to ruin.

What good is an afterlife without the Doctrine, without a dedicated army of light? If the Family is not purely militant in God's love, there is no point in ever leaving the bunker. It's not ideal, of course, but it's better than scrambling topside without conviction and allowing the Dark Prince to dilute Father Ernst's message. Preserving the Doctrine, even as a lived moment in time, as a purely historical pulse, is victory. Why can't they understand?

Even now, safe in his room, when Ernst visualizes the moment of unsealing—bunker door swung wide, light filling his eyes—his palms sweat. His limbs tremor. Unbidden, he sees riot police, SWAT team with snipers surrounding him. His old prison life comes at him hard—the brutality of men locked into bullpens, seething—and he can't go back to that. He won't. Truth be known, it's the only reason he does not commandeer the door when the Provider leaves on mission. He lurks in the tunnel, unbeknownst to them, ready to run for his secret crawlspace at a moment's notice.

Ernst swipes at his desk with an angry arm. Holy Bible, papers, a pen, clatter to the floor. Everything is slipping away. He has got to reign it back in. He needs Memaw Ruth's calm presence, but God won't let him speak with her. God is a brick wall, shutting him out.

"Father in Heaven, why?" Father Ernst clutches the framed photo of his first three wives. "Ruth," he cries, falling to his knees. There she is, smiling, beautiful as ever, gracious and kind. He rocks back and forth, tapping the picture against his forehead, harder and harder, until the glass breaks. Shards fall to the floor and sprinkle his face, his robe. He grips the frame until it snaps. Blood beads on his forehead, his hands. He opens his mouth to keen. The sound is primal and echoes off the walls.

Father Ernst wakes on the floor in a dusting of glitter. He is inside the snow globe dream. He struggles to sit, notices cuts on his hands. His head stings. He is in his chamber. Blood. Glass. Oh yes, the picture frame. Yes.

Ernst wipes his hands on the dirty robe and staggers upright. His body aches, his head thrums with a percussive beat. Memaw is gone, it's clear. Their only daughter, Ruth, forsaken. He must replace them. There's no time to waste.

He stretches his arms overhead, then drops them as he bends his knees, a few times over. He draws invisible circles in the air with his arms fully extended, clockwise, counter-clockwise. He hangs at the waist and slowly rolls up, undulates his spine. His exercise routine has diminished over the years, but he must keep the blood circulating. Waking the body also wakens the mind. Leadership requires a level of physical fitness and mental alertness unrecognized by most. Plus, he must be in good form tonight. He will take the Seventh.

Ernst reviews his assets: meat for a few days and not much water, aside from his private supply. Other than himself, only the builder knew about the hidden quarters adjoining his chamber, and the builder is long dead. It was a shame, however necessary. Ernst liked the man—brilliant, attentive, and a sworn devotee. Now, human resources in the bunker are slim: Silas will keep the lights on another few days, then provide for the others. Silas, Ernst's shadow, is weak—no charisma, no strength or prowess or ingenuity—but he does what he's told. He is no threat. Susan does what others are too squeamish for. Hannah and Ruth will keep as his wives and will be put to work. The children's value comes in relation to the Doctrine. They've been raised with it; they are his flock.

If the other cousin returns, Ernst will deal with him. In fact, he'll be disappointed if that black-haired traitor expires topside. Ernst wants to fight, needs to win something tangible to help keep focus.

Ernst hears benches scraping the floor and the muted hush of children's voices whispering in the Great Hall. So soon? The clock he relies on, the one he winds each night, is silent. He shakes it, but the second hand is frozen in time. He must have collapsed and lain on the floor all night, not just for a few moments as he thought—very disorienting. He was sure he had hours to prepare before the others even got out of bed.

He will have to make do.

He steps through the pile of debris, winces. He's cut his bare foot. Hops to the bedside and sits to look at the damage. One shard of glass protrudes from the yellowed ball, right through the tough old skin. Large enough to see easily, he still can't pull it with his fingers. He needs tweezers or a needle. "Rebekah," he calls in a hoarse voice. It's a moment before he remembers she is gone. He doesn't want Susan here; she's too clumsy. Hannah. He can't bear the girl to see him so vulnerable; she capitalizes on it.

He grimaces as his full weight bears down. He opens his door, turns to check the state of his room—a mess, Susan will have to clean it right away—and enters the hall, locking the door behind him.

The children sit at the table and pull Martyr cards. Movement and whispers, stilled to silence; they stare at him.

"Children," he booms. "Who's missing? Quickly, gather round. Silas, come. Mother Susan, ring the bell. I bring tidings of joy!" Purpose fuels him, and he laughs, touching their small heads.

Susan stands, hands on hips, glaring. She takes the bell from its place on the wall and clangs once, twice, then hangs it back up. Ruth appears from the shadows, shuffling her feet. Hannah arrives last, wrapped in a red shawl. She lifts her cheek for a kiss and sits at his left hand, bumping the children down the bench to make room.

Father Ernst says, "We are God's Army."

The children say, "We are the Light."

"We are the future."

"We pledge our life to God."

"We know the presence of Christ expels the presence of Satan. Whenever two or three are gathered together in His name, He is in their midst."

"Amen," they say.

"We have had our share of struggle. We have fought with the Devil, topside in the world and below, in our own hearts. But today we celebrate. We strengthen our commitment to God and to the Doctrine by calling upon the most sacred of vows and ushering them forth."

Hannah cocks her head, curious. Susan slouches behind the children, arms crossed. Ruth mouths something to Silas. She's not even listening.

"Cousins! It is time for me to take the Seventh. Children, you must wash and dress in your best and practice the Union Hymn. You have only heard it once. Silas, teach them. Mother Hannah, you will prepare Cousin Ruth for the ritual. You are cousins, and you will be like sisters as you share the motherdress and all it's responsibilities. Susan, I'll need you in my chamber, then preparing the feast. Silas, set the furniture for our ritual."

"Now?" says Ruth.

"Tonight you shall become my wife," he says.

"I'm not ready, Father," says Ruth. Her throat works and her cheeks flush. She looks to either side, but no one speaks.

"Cousin Hannah will help you, and we will all rejoice," he says.

Hannah opens her mouth, snaps it shut. She wheels toward Ruth.

"Must it really be tonight?" Ruth's voice is almost lost, it is so small.

Father Ernst steps closer. He lifts her hands to kiss her fingers. "This is God's Word. It shall be done."

"Amen."

CHAPTER 30

The old goat. Susan slaps a wet cloth and wipes the table with a violence that turns the children skittish. "Go on," she hisses. "Find Silas and do as he says."

The twins help Leah and Abel off the bench, and the whole lot hustles away.

For once Susan slept soundly, resting in preparation for this terrible new task—dispatching the children to God's garden. And now Father Ernst announces another wedding. This is the limit. Surely Memaw would not approve.

"Guide him, Mother Ruth," she whispers to the ceiling. "He has truly lost his way."

The doorknob rattles, and Father Ernst's door swings open. "Mother Susan, come." He waves. "Leave that, the others can do it."

"What others?" she mutters. But she abandons the rag. She has her own call of duty now, and it will take every bit of her strength to see it through.

He is flushed with excitement, eyes darting. He claps his hands once she passes in. Susan is wary but not frightened—which is something, given her last visit. She is in no mood for his tricky talks or his shifting temper. For the first time in all these years, she sees him as he really is: misguided and infantile. Ludicrous. Susan's lip curls in disgust. A familiar voice—Memaw Ruth's?—urges caution: *He's dangerous, still.*

Father Ernst strides past, saying something about the feast.

"What feast? There's only what's left of your daughter."

Father Ernst lunges. There is a tinkling sound. Now she sees the broken glass. He's standing in it, oblivious.

"Father, come away from that mess. Let me sweep it."

"What did you say?" His voice is hoarse. He runs a hand through his dishevelled hair until it stands on end. His beard glitters with more slivers of glass.

"Unless you mean to wait for the Provider," she adds. "Mayhap he'll bring root vegetables and some greens. That could make a good meal." *Stay calm*, says the voice—she could swear it is her old friend.

"It's only a thought, Father," she says. "Start your bath. I'll be back with the broom." She shuts the door behind her firmly.

If only there were a bolt on the outside. She'd close him in and tend to her greater task. It must be God's bidding. She'd never be bold enough to think that up on her own. Imagine, after all this time, God choosing to speak to *her*, a limping wreck of woman, overlooked most of her life. Despised, more like. To her, and *not* to the great Father Ernst.

Blessed are the meek, for they shall inherit the earth. So Memaw repeated often enough, and she would lock eyes with Susan as she said it. There was something in that, something hidden in the plainness of the statement pushing Susan to wonder. Shall they really? In this lifetime, the earth is lorded over by politicians, military men, lawyers, and priests. Rich, violent men—not one of them could be called meek, unless that word meant something very different in the time of Christ.

Father Ernst, as far from meek as they come.

Think, Susan. Memaw's voice, again. Susan feels the cool press of Memaw's hand on her sleeve.

Father Ernst promises they will inherit God's Garden, not *the earth.* Are they the same thing? Thorns and thistles, this is a slippery path she is on. Her mind churns and spits and worries like an old engine. No one else is in the Great Hall, just Susan, alone. She can almost see a filmy shift of Memaw herself. Memory? Susan reaches, and her hand goes right through the shimmering image.

Of course. She shakes her head. She's malnourished, dehydrated. Seeing things—it happens to them all. But the light pressure on her forearm persists. Now there is a small crowd waiting. Memaw, Deborah, Mary, and Rebekah. Susan extends her hand once more. Who is more long-suffering than these women? Christ—maybe. But as far as Susan knows, He was not defiled nightly nor forced into endless pregnancies, birthing in conditions worse than the animals they tended above ground. He was born suchly. He did not do the bearing.

"Susan!" Father Ernst bellows from the doorway. "The water's down. Get the kettle!"

Deborah rolls her eyes and Mary giggles. Memaw keeps her poise.

Susan whispers, "Please, let me come with you." How she misses them.

Soon. You still have work to do. Memaw points to Father's chamber, nodding.

Susan lights the stove and puts on a large pot of grey water to heat. An oil slick ripples on its surface, and slivers of lard soap slosh and float when she adjusts the pot on the element. It's not remotely clean, but even this water will improve Father Ernst. He has not washed in a very long time.

They shall hunger no more, neither thirst any more; neither shall the sun light upon them, nor any heat. Susan taps her fingers on the counter. She will wait one more day for God's new plan. Let the children have a Union feast, a song or two. Ruth will suffer tonight, but haven't they all? It seems to be God's design for women. Susan herself has done more than her share of lying down, spreading legs, being sexed upon command. It isn't what she'd want for a young girl, but this is the way of God's cruel world.

CHAPTER 31

Paul rests against rough bark, knees bent, feet fitted between gnarled roots that vein the dirt beneath the massive oak. Branches twist out of reach, like black arms stabbing the night. In every opening, the spackle of stars. A full and pitiless moon shines through foliage, lighting Thomas's handsome face and shaggy hair. Astounding, still, to look upon him. To hear his breath going in and out—Thomas's lungs, Thomas's hands and feet. His thumping chest, also full of hope and lies. A breeze drafts over Paul's skin, raising tiny hairs. It brings the scent of pine and campfire smoke and the rich musk of the earth. Under that, the tang of Thomas's humans—a hint of sweat and urine, their bodies now tucked beside the fire, resting. They are less strange to him already. Although Paul was shocked when Diego crept over to kiss Thomas goodnight. On the lips. Right in front of him. The kinship of lovers—bonds so deep Paul has never observed and only recently began to feel with Rebekah—unite the two men.

"Surprised?" Thomas's smirk unsettles him.

"No," Paul lies. "Yes. Actually." His mind reels. He tries to focus on the bigger situation, which is somehow less confusing. Paul is a hostage, after all. He shakes his tied wrists. "Cousin, is this really necessary?"

"Don't call me that."

Moonlight drips along the barrel of Paul's Ruger, which lies across Thomas's lap. "We both know you can work that loose, but rope will at least slow you down. What if you make a move for the gun and shoot me? Kill Diego and Sondra? Maybe you'd get back to the bunker in time to open the gun vault and arm the Family. That's not a risk I'm willing to take."

Shoot Thomas? Paul would sooner slit his own throat. "Don't know where the vault is."

"You never looked?"

Paul shakes his head "Must be inside Father Ernst's chamber. Never been in there. Door's always locked." A far-off call splits the night. Wild dog or coyote. Maybe a wolf. "Thomas, I'm not a believer."

"Good. You're still not one of us."

"Us, huh? How'd you meet them? Were you a prisoner, too?"

"Better. Took me for a lover." Thomas smiles, toothy and free. Full of mystery.

Rebekah took Paul, surely. Set her mind to it, came to him in the night. She unlocked a secret window, one that let in a gentle gust that touched every part of him inside and taught him how to feel again. Everything Paul learns about love contradicts Father Ernst's pronouncements. As far as Paul knows, it's the woman who decides what she wants, when, and with whom. Now he is seeing for himself that love does not even require a man and a woman. This simple truth makes room for itself inside his mind and inside his body, somewhere near his guts—how could Father Ernst, so worldly and learned, how could the whole world *not* know it, too?

This kind of thing he couldn't talk about with anyone, except maybe Thomas in the old days. After going to ground, that's who he'd looked to, not Jeremiah, Ernst's Second. Jeremiah established a pecking order amongst the boys putting Thomas at the bottom—some twisted sibling rivalry. Jeremiah had the best bunk, the warmest corner. He made Thomas, who never pushed for attention, hang curtains to mark his territory, make his bed, complete all his chores. Jeremiah was the most like Father Ernst of them all, and had been set apart and mentored. It was a great loss when he died.

"What do you really know about them, Thomas?"

"Sondra was a student before. She's read a forest of books and lived through a lot too. Diego worked with undocumented farm workers, fighting for their rights."

Of all the stars in the sky, the one Paul wishes on must be the least significant. He can't even fathom a world of book reading and writing, of life saving.

"When did you stop believing?"

Paul supposes Thomas won't answer, the way he squirms, but a moment later he speaks. "When you're little, you don't know any better. Father Ernst is like God. Everybody listening, wanting to be like him. My brothers worshipped him, and look what happened—he sent them to their deaths, other than Jeremiah. I couldn't stand hearing those sermons any more. Inside, I knew I was different." Thomas's voice is softer, his words more considered than when his friends are present.

Paul leans forward. "Why didn't you stay and challenge him?"

"I argued with him. His wrath was unbelievable. If I'd stayed, he would've gotten rid of me somehow. What good would I be dead?"

Paul's chest tightens when he whispers, "You abandoned us."

"Who could I trust? Jeremiah turned me over to Ernst every chance he got. I was whipped for a week straight. Still got the scars. You were young, busy playing soldier."

Paul nods. He's had his own problems, trying to reason with Ruth. She'd sooner give him a Curing, let Father literally cut open his gullet and pluck out the black seed of doubt, than turn against the Family.

Thomas stretches his legs, tilts his head back to look up. "Rest. We're heading out soon, and we want to get there before noon. You'll go in first, I'll follow. They'll cover the entrance and the tunnel. We won't hurt anyone who doesn't fight."

"All they know down there is the Devil that Father speaks of. They fear everyone, everything. They're bound to fight from sheer terror."

"That's why you'll talk to them first, calm them down. We'll protect any who join us. I'll go straight for Ernst. We need him alive—got it?"

Paul nods.

"We could have driven right up to the door, days ago," Thomas is saying. "But we were taking precautions. Wanted to scout out the forest. Had no idea what to expect from the locals."

If they had driven directly to the compound, Paul might have never met them. Or might not have even left yet on his mission. He says, "Military station came down about four months ago. Probably gave up on us by now. Neighbours are scattered, who knows where."

"How many men in the bunker?"

"Father, of course. There's Cousin Silas, younger'n me. And wee Abel. He's two, I think. Three."

"That's it?"

"Jeremiah got gruesome ill soon after we thought you'd died."

"There must be babies. Other toddlers?"

Paul stares at Thomas. Says nothing. Finally, Thomas looks away. He shudders.

But Paul worries about the women, other than Rebekah. Ruth is more a fighter than all the boys combined. Always glorifying the Martyrs and quick with her knife. Mother Susan—who knows what she's capable of.

Thomas says, "You might think it was easy, but leaving was terrifying. I was on the run a long time. Left the state, hoped no one would recognize me. Had a hard time fitting in. I was avoiding people, stealing or foraging food, sleeping rough. Didn't trust anyone. The only people who talked to me were as bad or worse than Ernst. They claim to be all kinds of Christian, but so many are full of hate, Paul. They wanted me to fight on their side but didn't want to know the real me. I'm through with those lies. I tried to block out all the garbage we learned, you know, but it's hard. A hymn comes whistling out, or something from the Doctrine, when I least expect it."

"Why'd you come back here?"

"Oh. When I met Diego, I really fell for him. I didn't know he was part of the resistance. Sondra thought I was undercover, trying to infiltrate. I had to tell them the truth, who I was. Took a long time for them to trust me. But Diego kept thinking about the bunker, kept asking questions. I figured the Family'd be dead by now." Thomas looks down and traces the length of the Ruger with a finger. "I guess part of me needed to know what happened to everyone." He looks at Paul carefully. "And I want Diego to know all of me, who I used to be, and where I grew up. They might seem scary, but these are good people, Paul. More family than I had on the Farm. They want justice and, eventually, peace. Ernst's weapons could help make that happen. Capturing Ernst is an added bonus."

Paul bites his lip hard. How can Thomas battle topside with strangers but not help his own kin in the bunker? "Why'd you get mixed up in their fight?"

"Paul, it's not *their* fight. It's all of ours. Ernst started a war, whether he meant to or not. Right-wingers mobilized fast—End of Dayers, militiamen, survivalists. We think the Family was just some isolated thing, but Ernst had connections all over. America was a time bomb, and he lit that fuse."

"Hard to imagine. I barely left the Farm, let alone the county." Paul pauses and looks at Thomas. "Do you think Father Ernst knew what would happen?"

"Who knows? It's not our fault, what he did. But it's our responsibility to help make it right. You going soft for him now?"

"Thomas, he murdered my father and called him a traitor. He lies and hurts us for no reason. Keeps us down there to control us. What he does to the girls, the women? I hate him. I hate him. You have no idea." Paul clenches his tied fists, rubs his face with the knotted rope.

"And that's how he treats his relations. Imagine what he's done to his enemies," says Thomas.

"I never seen him outside the Family."

"We don't have to live his lies anymore, but we've got to help undo the damage he caused."

An owl hoots, startling them. In the eerie silence after its call, Paul notices a thousand tiny hacksaws grinding. "Crickets?"

"Cicadas," Thomas says. "They go below ground for years at a time. Then one day, they crawl out of the dirt to lay eggs, unfurl their wings, and fly away."

Paul says, "Like us."

"Yes. Like us." Thomas points up. "Look at the moon. See how fast it walks? Time to wake them. Time to move out."

Paul cranes his neck and squints, but the fat moon doesn't appear to move, not even an inch. It hangs in the purple magic of that midnight sky, lighting the path before them.

CHAPTER 32

A memory: women pulling nightshirts over their heads, letting white cotton fall about their shoulders. Struggling, heads effaced, wings flapping for sleeve holes, dark, thatched armpits winking, pale torsos marked by wiry bush above dimpled legs. Susan's humped back, always distinctive. Cotton smoothed, bodies erased, they knelt for prayer. Murmurs of goodnight. The room felt full and safe at bedtime. After the last one dropped, Memaw would put out the light.

Ruth stares at the mattress airing against the wall, covered by a sheet, and at Rebekah's empty bedframe. The other cots are made up, covered in grey blankets. She wishes to be folded and stacked neatly with the linens, weighed down by rough wool, ignored at the foot of an iron-framed bed.

"Haul yourself," says Hannah.

Ruth collapses on her mattress in silence. Why did she think she could escape this fate? No one else had.

"It's not so bad," says Hannah. "You get extras. Father is a lot nicer when you're a wife. Mostly."

Ruth can hardly swallow for the sticking in her throat.

"What're you worried about? I'm the one who'll have to work now. I haven't even produced." Hannah's voice falters. Ruth looks up at her cousin. Hannah is rarely without a confident sneer—bossing the younger girls, snubbing the mothers, flirting behind Father Ernst's back with the boys. She whispers, "I failed."

"It's not your fault, Hannah. We're too skinny, Susan said so. She hasn't carried a baby to term since the twins."

"Why does Father think you'll be fertile? Whatever gave him that idea?"

"God's truth, I don't know." He spoke of their great renaissance, of Memaw's legacy passing through Ruth to the next generation. It sounded like wild talk to Ruth, like wishful thinking.

The girls face one another. Hannah's always been prettiest, but even she is sallow, gaunt. Eyes peer from dark circles, teeth are loose and yellowed. Her hair is listless and greasy but, unlike the others, not thinning as much along the part. She's had more to eat.

"What must I do?" Ruth's finger traces a seam on her bedcover.

"In the ritual? Say the pledge, say 'I do.' Father does most of the talking."

Ruth shakes her head. "After. In the chamber."

Hannah laughs abruptly. "Whatever he says. If you're smart, you try things."

"Things?"

"Things you've wondered about. Between a man and woman. He's happy when you try."

Ruth gasps. "I cannot."

"Oh, you can. Close your eyes and pretend it's someone handsome. It's your only job, may as well be good at it." Hannah shrugs. "Besides, you get treats."

The sugar cube. Ruth swallows. "I'd rather be a ratsticker."

"You look like one. Comb out your hair. And wash between your legs. Are you still bleeding?"

Ruth shakes her head.

"Good, Father can't abide that mess."

Girl whispers. Leah and the twins come in. They strip and leave clothes in piles on the floor. They pull out their best dresses. Hannah helps, for once. She fluffs the thin, patched skirts and begins braiding Leah's hair. She ties little ribbons in place. "Go on," she says. She tosses a towel to Ruth.

Ruth paces the shower room's cold floor. This is happening. Her legs tremble, and her knees are watery. She believed Paul would save her. He tried. They sat at the cairn the night before he left. Paul held her chin and said, "May as well slit your belly as stay. We got to go up, Ruth."

She was shocked. "We Ascend when the time is right. When Father says. Not when we're fearful or desolate."

"Come with me."

"For shame, girls can't," she said, although a thrill heated her. "Though foraging is better than being a cousin mother ..."

He said, "Not to scavenge. I mean to live. Permanently."

"Blasphemer! Topside, they hate us. The bunker will inherit the earth. You must have faith. You must believe!"

"Father Ernst can't make me and neither can you."

"Shush, Paul." How frightened she was, covering his mouth with shaking fingers. "What will Father say?"

Paul took her hands and held them. He touched one finger to the thin skin of her chest below the collarbone, where her heart should be. It unhinged her. He said, "Father Ernst is a liar. A murdering raper. Know what that means? I don't want that for you. Us leaving has to be a secret."

A sob caught in her throat. Paul was tainted, the Devil had taken his spirit. Like their father, fallen to evil. Yet—*the humping grind*—she'd seen Father Ernst do that to Hannah. Who would ever want that?

At last she said, "We'd marry, you and me, topside?" There was that picture again: flowers in her bridal veil, the clasping of hands, the singing of vows.

"What?" Paul shook his head. "You're ... a kid."

"I'm not!"

"You're my *sister*."

"There are no brothers and sisters, Father Ernst said so. We are all cousins, now and forever. We could homestead. I could keep you."

"No, Ruth."

Once, Ruth dropped a pebble down the cistern. That was her belly: the long-drop wait and finally pain, landing with a splash. *Am I not yours?* she longed to shout as her dream broke open and fell about in pieces.

"I promised our dad to protect you." Paul wiped his face with his sleeve. "We can camp in the forest like we used to. Like he taught us."

The hurt of rejection stung, gathered momentum, and hissed between her teeth. "Like traitors. Like infidels? I won't leave my people."

Now, on the cusp of becoming a cousin-bride, she could see that Paul had been clear. He had not led her on, not once. Had only ever tried to keep her safe from harm. It was Ruth's great imagination, her yearning, which filled the empty space between what *was* and what *might* be. It flourished in that great void—furtive and fearful, with those other unvoiced hungers.

A child in the doorway startles her. "Blessed Flowering, Mother Ruth," says Rachel. She kisses Ruth's cheek. "We got the bridal gown out. It's pretty. Hannah says you're to come get dressed." Ruth hasn't even started washing. She drags out the grey-water bucket and dunks a rag. "I'll be there soon enough," she says, and steps out of her pants, her leggings, her socks. When Rachel is gone, she hoists her skirt and begins to bathe.

CHAPTER 33

Father Ernst grips the podium. He's wearing a slightly cleaner gown with the ministry shawl, gold-embroidered with the Family insignia. Susan helped with his room and also with his hair, his beard. It is trimmed somewhat, and she combed the glass shards out. He looked good when he checked the small mirror hanging on his chamber wall.

Ruth trembles before him, her mother's green comb in her sparse hair. The bridal gown sags open at her neck. There's the whiter ring of her throat where she washed with a damp cloth and the grime below that line—her collar and shoulder bones perch above non-existent décolletage. The girls have tried to stitch the fabric down to fit her better. Pins glint, here and there, where they ran out of time to sew. The waist is wrapped with a pale sash, extra fabric folded in behind. Painted Mason jar screw-top lids for bracelets. Father Ernst hesitates. She looks even more a child in this oversized dress.

He remembers coming in from the barn, scraping mud and manure from his heels, stepping out of his boots, and opening the back door. Sock feet silenced his entrance to Deborah's kitchen. Hand on the knob, body frozen in shock while he struggled to make sense of the scene unfolding before him. The kids were playing dress-up, clomping on the linoleum in Deborah's modest pumps. The toddler, Rebekah, was swimming in Deborah's party dress, clutching a shiny purse. She chucked paper confetti at the other two. Deborah's eldest daughter, that heretic, wore Ernst's good suit with cufflinks and a tie. She had drawn a moustache under her nose and swaggered, holding the family Bible, mimicking him. Who was the pretty bride holding the sagging bustier with one hand, suffocating a bouquet of wildflowers under her bare arm, wedding veil tucked into curled blond hair? Mincing and cooing and fluttering long lashes—it was none other than Thomas, their youngest boy. Sacrilege. Obviously the girl had orchestrated it. She had painted their lurid makeup, styled their hair, got them into the grownups' clothes in the first place. That Jezebel took a whipping for it, right after the boy. The rage that transported Ernst left marks on their skin for years. Deborah wept and tried to intervene, but he would not be placated. "It's unnatural," he shouted. "Where were you to let the Devil enter my house and poison my children?" He whipped her too, and forced the devastated children to watch. She prayed as he hit, even when it broke the skin, finally speaking in tongues in a gnashing frenzy before collapsing on the floor while the children clung to one another, sobbing.

Father Ernst hears the shuffling of small feet, a rattling cough from the benches. He blinks. The Great Hall. A small gathering. He's at the pulpit. How long has he been standing here? He searches out Susan's grim face. A young bride bites her lip. The Union ceremony. Yes. He holds the girl's hands, kisses her cheeks, forehead, and last, presses his mouth to hers. The girl leans away, even as he pulls her closer. She's holding her breath. His moustache bristles against her skin, his beard catches in the gape of her dress. Hot breath whistles out his nostrils, tickling the wiry hairs. When he lets go, the girl gasps. She will have to learn to kiss better.

"Kneel." She lowers herself to the Vestal Cushion. The Seventh, that's right.

Father Ernst clears his throat. "Today we give thanks and celebrate. I have guarded our Cousin's innocence, as I guard you all, awaiting this day to stake my claim. God says the Seventh will bring abundance and joy. She shall provide for us all—children to fill our home, to rebuild our church. Soldiers, for God's great army. How do we pledge?"

The children say, "We give ourselves to God."

"Let us raise our voices, that God hear our prayers."

"We lift them up unto the Lord."

"Let us sing!"

"Cousins shall seed and breed and feed, and one day die in glory!"

"Amen. Now the time is come for the Initiation. Woman's modest duty—to humbly serve both man and God in purity of Thought, Word, and Deed. To reject Satan and sinful pleasure, though the Dark Prince may try to tempt her. Let us sing together the words our Father taught us:

"Blessed be the mother
Chaste in body, pure in mind
She that humbly beseeches God
Watch over her

Provide an earthly steward
Watch over her
A husband, the one true path
Watch over her.

"Very good. And I say women who do not revoke Satan are not women at all. They are a devil-rotting witchery, unworthy of my love. Cousin mothers, noble arms in waiting, bosom soldiers of God, shall never mix with demon flesh, that which parades as female but holds the dragon's key to sin's lock, and turns it as she likes."

Father Ernst glares at the small congregation. The youngest children gape, fuelling him.

"Cousin Bride. Are you free of shame burdens? Are you ready and worthy of my Claim?"

"I am, I hope," Ruth peeps. Her eyes dart around.

"And do you accept your sworn wifely duties?

"I do."

"And will you forsake all others?"

"I w-will," she stammers. Wipes her palms on the skirt.

"You are sworn by the divine rights given me by God Himself. I declare you Cousin Bride, Seventh of my Holy tribe. Praise be." Father Ernst leans close and seizes her waist. A sharp pin jabs, and he hisses. A drop of his blood on the once-white cloth. "Thorns on my new rose," he says. He presses his mouth on her again. He will show her what a kiss is.

The children say, "Praise be."

He shouts, "Let us feast!"

Father points to the bench on his left, and Ruth slides in. He pats down her billowing skirts and rests his hand on her quavering thigh. Hannah, sulking, serves a meagre bit of water, and Susan limps after with the warm bowls. Ruth gets a large portion, oat gruel with the oily meat. She stares at it. Looks up at him, looks away.

So tiresome. At least the others begin to eat.

"Wife, you will need your energy tonight. Eat up!" Father Ernst laughs, but no one joins in. What a dreary bunch. "This is supposed to be a celebration," he says. "Finish your food. Then we must sing, Cousins!"

The others scrape bowls with their spoons. The dishes clatter when Hannah and Susan collect them. "The Wedding Hymn," shouts Father. "Have you young ones learned it? Silas, lead them."

Silas pushes the twins beside Abel and Leah. "Together first, then in rounds," he says. He claps to count them in.

Such harmonies—mostly all the right notes, not bad for an hour or two of practice. Strange, he never noticed how mournful this song sounds. Memaw wrote it for Deborah's wedding, sitting at the church piano one morning. It had been sung at each Union ritual since.

"Again," he shouts. "This time, we will dance."

The littlest one, the girl, curtseys and hops but tires quickly. The twins encircle the little boy, and he stamps his foot off-time. Silas hovers beside Hannah, no doubt hoping she will take him in hand. She doesn't. She's pouting, arms crossed, won't look Father Ernst in the face, won't look at Ruth either. She will learn to fall in line.

"Come, my Bride! The wedding waltz." Father Ernst extends his hand. It starts off poorly, gets worse. She stumbles on his feet, tramples the hem of her gown. When he leads left, she careens into him. When right, she bangs her head on his shoulder, looking the wrong way. She did not practice, obviously.

"Relax," he says into her hair. "You must learn to follow me. I am your God, your Master." He spins her around; her braids twirl. One, two turns—the girl reddens and begins to cough.

"Please," she says. She is winded.

"There, there," he says, "that will do." He holds her close. His chuckled baritone should soothe her, but she pulls away, still coughing. He clamps onto her, gets pricked with another needle. "Damn!" Father Ernst licks his lips. Half moons from his sharp nails press into her arms. His hands tighten around her waist, then slide down to cup her buttocks through the gown. Fingers knead her flesh. There is something underneath her dress—what?

The girl steps back to face him. A nervous smile.

"Again," he says. He presses the length of his body against her, takes up her left hand in his right. He steps, counting out loud. "One-two-three, one-two-three. See? It's not too hard." His hips move against her, eyes wrinkle shut. Although her limbs are plain enough, he is roused by the excitement of the day, by the clumsy dance. So many things must be shown to her. It all begins tonight.

CHAPTER 34

Should have slept while he had the chance. The blisters on Paul's feet chafe and bleed into the boots, and his calf muscles cramp. His stamina, already compromised, is waning. He cannot keep up with Thomas and his friends, who lope through the forest as silent and graceful as the animals watching from the shadows. The full moon hangs low in the sky, lighting their passage, but he can barely make out their silhouettes, so far ahead. Whenever the treetops' leafy splendour overtakes or clouds pass in front of the powerful orb, Paul is lost. He trips on a root, smacking face-first into thick and twisted branches. Cobwebs ghost across his face, and the frantic scrambling of tiny legs causes him to shudder, to bat the insects away with his thin arms. He half hopes to lose the rebels, to be left on his own, for good.

The Family, paralyzed and toxic, has no future. He knows this as well as his own name. Thomas might not even need Paul to get cooperation from the others. They'll be shocked to see him alive, for starters. Plus they're desperate for food and water: they need help. Diego has promised medical attention, protection, and a safe place for the children to recuperate. They'd be better off with Thomas's people than scrounging a meagre forest life with Paul. If it weren't for Rebekah, Paul would tear away right now and hide in the black woods. He could eke out a basic survival—or not. For once it wouldn't matter, with no one else depending on him. He'd be accountable only to himself, allowed to fail or even abstain from trying: its own kind of freedom.

Giving up. That's exhaustion talking. Paul can almost hear his father's voice, chiding. Yet isn't that what Thomas did when he escaped—surrender to an unlikely future? Thomas cast himself out into a world of violence and treachery, yet he lives. Alone in the wild, he was reduced to gleaning among the sheaves for survival, was despised and rejected, and then transformed, rose up, and returned, cloaked in mystery, full of purpose. Like metal forged from an ancient fire, Thomas, reborn, cuts through confusion and so many lies. Just like His Holy blade of Truth in the Doctrine.

Who is Paul without Ruth, whose very existence defines him? Orphan, brother, guardian. Or without Rebekah, who has made it all bearable with the recent gift of her love? An invisible pendulum seeks balance: heavy burdens weigh in against a few quick moments of joy, the wonder of possibility. If he gives up one, will he lose the other? Who would he even be, minus Father Ernst's oppressive yoke chaining him in place? Like pedalling the bunker's stationary bike; if it were plucked out and set free by God's hand, where would he ride?

Paul freezes, pulse in his throat. Trees surround him: silent accusations. The trail made by the others is nowhere to be seen. Distracted, he has crept off-course, twice in as many days. Abandonment, that old fear, consumes, and a rush of futility floods him. He wished for independence earlier, and now? Paul scurries in one direction, then its opposite. Another gossamer web pulls at his forehead and across his cheek, and he panics. Bends at the waist to shake out his hair—could be a black widow crawling in there. Then, a familiar sound: chuckling. Paul wheels around, gasping. It's Sondra, the stealthy huntress.

He who loves nature, the Family's best forager, is losing his nerve. "Thought you were up ahead," he mumbles.

"Just making sure you aren't snake bait, again." The dips of facial contours, the hollow workings of her throat, hum with the moon's silver light.

Paul tries to smile, but the joke digs. Before these rebels appeared, he was in good control of himself. He had plans and hopes and, most of all, confidence in his own skills. He was going to save the Family, or die trying.

"You okay?" she asks, touching him.

He flinches.

"We're almost there. Got to make it past the dead zone. We hid our truck in an old barn."

"We're not walking back across the sands?"

"God, no. That would take a day or more," she laughs.

Paul does not join in.

"Sorry. That must sound bratty. I guess you've only been on foot."

"Yes." He can still feel the heat from her hand where she placed it on his shoulder.

"Come," she says. She smiles—she, who might have killed him only the day before, whose eyes first set upon his like a predator's. Paul's throat sticks with an unknown emotion.

Paul follows her and the forest thins. They work their way

through the most drought-damaged section—the southern tip, nearest the Great Standoff's local bombing site. He'd never come this far on his foraging missions, and for good reason. Dead and dying trees, as far as he can see, are dusted in ash. Sondra ties a rag over her mouth and gestures with her hands: don't touch. His UV hood, gas mask, and gloves would be useful now, but Thomas took them, along with Paul's rifle. Paul copies Sondra, and they pick their way with slow intent, stepping in tracks left by Diego and Thomas, trying not to stir up the dust. Who knew if it was still toxic? They move as one, helping each other climb and balance and scale the downed logs. When she leans into him, he absorbs her weight, buoying her slight frame. When he must press back, her strength surprises him.

Carnage, that's what they trek through in the pre-dawn light. Tree corpses, staggering and broken open, branches helter-skelter, pointing sun-bleached fingers of blame. This act, witnessing, chokes the spark of hope buried deep inside and threatens to undo him. Like in the *Book of Matthew*, he feels he has been thrown into the furnace of fire with much weeping and gnashing of teeth. The whole time, it is the slope of Sondra's back, the determined set of her shoulders, that keeps him moving forward until, finally, they break from ghostly brambles and reach an old fence line with untilled land on the other side.

Thomas and Diego dig with a trowel from their kit, right beside one of the old fence posts. They each wear one of Paul's gloves. Diego has the gas mask and Thomas the veiled hood.

"Slow pokes," says Thomas.

"Here we go," says Diego. He unearths a package. Inside is a gun, bullets, a bottle of water, meal replacement bars, and a cellphone. "We stashed this on the way in."

Paul hasn't seen a cellphone in years. Before they went to ground, all of the men carried them, and each of the wives had one for emergencies. Father Ernst forbade them in the bunker, fearing they could be tracked, and he was right. It's how the FBI discovered some of the other settlements.

Paul says, "Aren't they illegal?"

Thomas laughs. "*We* are illegal." He opens one of the bars, takes a large bite, and passes it to Diego.

"Burners are hard to get on the black market," says Diego.

"The white market," says Sondra, smirking. She drinks from the water bottle and trades it for another of the bars.

"Most carriers went bankrupt or dissolved after the legislation passed," says Diego, patiently. "Like internet providers, it's all government regulated."

"Only the big wigs get them, officially," says Thomas.

"Unless you can hack," says Sondra. She is already removing tiny, inscrutable pieces and switching them out for bits she carried in her pocket. She texts a cryptic message—signs and symbols—and presses send.

Hack. What does that even mean? Paul rubs his head, which throbs from the hit he took in the forest and the earlier blows dealt by Sondra. He drinks from the bottle. Bites into one of the bars and chews slowly: fruit of some kind, nuts, and seeds. Could that be honey? He hasn't tasted anything so sweet in a very long time; the sugar rush energizes and helps him focus.

Thomas loads the pistol and tucks it in the waistband of his pants, nestled against the small of his back. Paul's Ruger leans where Thomas left it, against a fence post, looking forlorn. Paul hasn't so much as touched it since encountering the group. His hands itch for its reassuring weight. He feels vulnerable, less able to defend himself without it. And he misses the connection to his father, which imbued a sense of confidence he's been lacking.

"Good to go," says Sondra. "Should have some backup by nightfall." She is already fiddling with the phone again, changing the tiny pieces inside. "We can rest in the barn until then."

"Should we wait that long?" Paul's belly tightens with a sense of urgency. Anything could have transpired in the bunker since he left.

"Relax. After all these years, a few hours isn't going to make much difference," says Thomas. "Better to be rested." He takes a long pull from the water bottle, his throat bobbing with each swallow.

Paul strides into the field, but Diego pulls him back sharply. "Landmines, kid. Be careful."

Kid. Paul has lost all of his good sense. He shuffles behind the rest of them, humiliated, as they creep through tall grass that grows up and around the downed trunks of countless destroyed trees. As he steps over and around decaying logs, Paul detects the tiny movements of beetles. Tracks lead to and from the large trunks. Even after death, the trees support a small, miraculous universe.

Soon, in the near distance, Paul can make out the shape of a dilapidated barn. They stop for more water and Sondra says, "Our truck's inside." He stares for a long time. Could that have been the Andersons' place? If so, he knows the derelict highway is just beyond.

Thomas says, "I trust you won't blow our heads off," and passes the Ruger back to Paul, who beams. He strokes the smooth laminate and automatically checks that it's loaded, that the safety is on. He feels taller again, shifting to adjust for the added weight when he slings it over his shoulder.

The road was relinquished decades ago to farm machinery and horse-pulled wagons once the newer, paved bypass took most traffic with it. The old road mimics the curves of the river and the once proud forest. It leads north past an unmarked lane—the private entrance to the Family's compound—and south, to whatever is left of the town. This is the same road he set out on days ago, just a few miles up ahead. Paul has almost come full circle.

CHAPTER 35

Susan slumps onto a bench after Hannah takes the children to bed. Cousin Silas hovers, glancing from kitchen to Susan, then to Father Ernst's door. "She'll be fine," Susan mutters. The boy blushes and disappears.

Susan is exhausted. She may not have enough energy to execute her plan. Poison would be easiest, possibly kindest, but they've nothing left in that department. She can repurpose cords or rope for a noose but hasn't the strength to hoist the bodies. Also she cannot erase the picture of Rebekah's damaged face—thickened tongue, bulging eye sockets, lips curled in anguish, and those terrible markings at her throat. She settles on knives. Fast and ungentle. She'll do the girls and Abel first. Severing the oesophagus kills almost instantly, but there will be a lot of blood. If she could do it to livestock, she can do the children. She likes animals better.

She flicks a spot of congealed grease on the table beside her hand. Spills rarely go unnoticed—the children will lick anything. Once it sets, even after scrubbing, such drops stain the otherwise unremarkable wood. Phantoms seeped into the polished grain under her fingers, the map of a thousand shared meals. She squints and it looks like flowers blooming on a vine, serrated-edge leaves with thorns and heart-shaped petals.

Will there be flowers wherever she ends up? Will she at least glimpse them when she clings for all eternity outside the gate to

God's Garden? That might be enough, to see and smell them, if not to touch. Why should the Afterlife be any less disappointing than this life she has crawled through, miserably?

She dunks her rag in the basin beside her. It's surprising the Family is able to make any mess at all, given so few provisions. Yet dust falls thick, now as ever. After today, it won't matter what state the place is in. Yet habit and a sense of duty prevails, so Susan wipes the scarred wooden table one last time. An arc of fire tongues her lower back when she reaches. She kneels to get in close for the overhang, the side panels, and wipes the sturdy legs, too. Since she's already down, she ducks her head under. No cobwebs, but something else catches her eye. A rough drawing—no, a carving: a heart with Paul's name spelled inside. Which of the hussies did this?

All the girls, even the little ones, flutter when he's near. Memaw doted on him, annoying Father Ernst to no end. Annoying Susan as well. Hannah makes no attempt to hide flirtations, and Ruth demonstrates a silent but fierce loyalty that rivals any hound's. What is it about the boy? Black hair, distinct from the others. She supposes he is kind. Hard to say. Mostly they mute themselves in the bunker, tamp down any excess of personality. Any outward show of feeling can be aired during Reflections and, more than likely, whipped out of them. Rebekah acted like a detached Missionary, but she was also drawn to Cousin Paul. That kind of affection is hard to name—one that pulses with magnetism and mystery. Could it have been more than friendship?

Footsteps. Susan is humped under the table and when she

moves, pain flares the length of her spine. She hopes it is Hannah and that the girl will help her up. It's Cousin Silas shuffling to the kitchen—he never lifts his feet. Drawers slide open, bump shut. He's rummaging, doesn't know his way around. Filching another morsel, no doubt. The boy is hopeless.

Susan presses palms to bench and tries to stand again. Her arms shake with effort. The left foot cramps, the whole leg is numb. "Come," she calls out when the boy re-enters the Hall. He freezes, caught.

"I'll not mention this trespass if you hurry up."

He blushes, looks to his hands, and she sees them—cleaver, carving knife, deboning knife, even the meat fork and scissors—anything with a blade or point.

"What are you doing, fool?"

The boy wavers. One step toward her, one back to the kitchen. "His blade of Truth?" he says, without conviction.

"Put those down! Help me."

His guilty face morphs to one of dread; the boy hates conflict. If he helps Susan, he'll have to set down the knives. If he sets them down, she'll grab them. He will have to fight her. His face says he can't.

"Good boy."

A sound escapes his round mouth, and he darts from the Hall. She is surprised that he disobeyed. Where the devil is he taking them? He's not an original thinker, so who put him up to this?

Ruth, of course. Or Hannah?

Susan presses weight into her palm on the bench, pulls with the other hand clutching the table edge. Sweat stands on her upper lip and pools between slack breasts. "Memaw, give me strength," she whispers. She's up, panting, right hip beached on wood. She points and flexes her toes to start the blood moving again. It takes time before she can stand and limp her way across the room. In a narrow drawer near the stove is the fourteen-inch chef's knife and sharpening stone, too long to fit the block with the others. "Blade of Truth indeed, stupid boy."

The twins and Leah are abed. No sign of Hannah. Susan rests on her cot, sets the knife and stone down. She had a whim to put the girls under one blanket so they'll arrive at the Garden together, but they're too heavy for her to lift. She pushes the cots together instead. Sits again to catch her breath. She begins to sharpen the blade, drawing it up the stone, flipping it, and drawing it up the other side. Kitchen music; she never tires of it. The twins stir and settle. She hardly ever thinks of them as her own. The birthing was hard, messy, but she gritted her teeth and pushed, Memaw and Deborah on either side, cheerleading. The babies looked strange—red-faced, mucous-plugged, placenta sheen glistening—but even in that barbaric state, she was secretly pleased. Finally, after so many miscarriages topside. Father Ernst praised her for bearing the first of the new tribe below—oh, how she was celebrated. She brought the twins forth, gave them life. Now she can guide them to the next. Better than delivering them to Father Ernst.

Helen sleeps on her back, arms and legs thrown wide. More authoritative, this one always grasps for facts, reason, rules. Rachel rolls on her side to face her twin. A freckle on her right earlobe—the only way Susan could tell them apart, at first. Rachel doesn't challenge her sister, doesn't encourage her, either. She reminds Susan of a mule they had topside, plodding the fields apart from horses and men, minding his own. A lot like Susan herself. On instinct, Helen inches toward Rachel's warmth. Her small chest rises and falls under the sheet. Susan could put a quilt over them.

She sets down the knife and stone, lifts the lid on Rebekah's old trunk—empty. Ruth sorted her things, but what became of that much fussed-over quilt? Fine handiwork, no doubt. She opens Ruth's trunk and it's there, under hand-me-down dresses. The last time she saw it, it was rough basted, pins everywhere, and still needed the final edging.

Susan unfolds it across the two cots, covering the girls. Unless Ruth had a peek, she's the first to see it. It's a complex scene she can't figure. Upside down. She shifts it the right way around. Sucks in her breath. Rebekah's finest work. Immaculate. Susan thumbs the stunning panels—chocolate-brown from Memaw's best housedress, gunmetal sashings from Deborah's overcoat lining, hints of midnight-blue from Mary's negligee. Mainly the colours of night, of the bunker itself—rusted pipe and scaling kettle, blackened oven, gleaming stove elements. Within the border, the top section lightens with pieces of that Floridian-orange apron, and cream-coloured slips, butter nightcaps, scraps of the children's Christening gowns. It's a sunrise, a sophisticated pinwheel pattern, made from items belonging to each of them. The corner blocks are stunning: meticulous appliqué and free-motion embroidery replicate familiar profiles. Memaw,

Deborah, Mary, and Susan herself. Astounding.

Least photogenic and most camera-shy of the wives, Susan rarely has had her picture taken, let alone a painstaking tribute made—like this. Susan cannot stop looking at the fourth corner: the image captures her likeness but is softer than she feels. Kinder. More dignified. Almost handsome. Like the woman she might have become, in other circumstances.

The embroidered centrepiece shows a robed, bearded man lying at the feet of a bride whose gown drips blood. The background is stitched in heavy thread—ladders, ladders everywhere. Susan flips a corner. On the plain backing, spidery red-threaded letters spell out *The Ascension Made Manifest*. The title of Father's Book of Sermons.

Rebekah's vision of the Ascension is shockingly different from Father's. Susan grips the foot rail of Helen's bed, sinks her weight onto it. She has not forgotten that heretic bonnet, some kind of infant's mourning cap, although she did not show it to Father Ernst or tell him what she discovered in her grisly work. What more could he do to punish a dead woman? Rebekah was probably about four months along, hence the moods, her frequent tears. *The poor girl*.

Susan's heart stutters, she can't get her breath. She eases herself onto the mattress. Clutches the knife, drops it.

Sacrilege, what Rebekah's done. Yet this was the same girl who gifted Susan a needlepoint replica of the Farm based on the photograph in Father's chamber—her most treasured possession. The Farm. That was what Susan loved and what she had been promised, not this filthy bunker living. A safe place to live and work.

And she was to be let alone, Memaw said.

Ernst. Without him, the women would still be alive. They'd be up on that big front porch rocking, sewing, laughing. Waiting for the bread to rise. Simmering soup, letting pies cool on the sill. Her mind jumps to Memaw's ghostly smile, her voice reminding Susan, *You still have work to do.* Susan imagined bolting Father Ernst inside his chamber earlier today, removing him from the picture entirely: heresy. Or simply another unexpected task required to ensure their survival?

It's not too late.

There's a shift inside her, an opening. Like hauling up a window that's been painted shut for so many years. Susan knows now what it is she must do.

"Mother Susan." Helen is awake.

Susan tucks the stone and knife into her apron pocket. "Come, child. I need your help moving the big table."

Susan stands, beckons. She steps once, twice, lurches on her bad side. Her slow legs are covered in bark. Her torso is the trunk. Arms, the spindling branches of an ancient tree. Sap runs in her veins, not blood. Susan stands between heaven and earth, connecting the two, and stars of the blackest night lodge in the leafy twigs of her hair.

CHAPTER 36

The king-size bed dominates the chamber. Even topside, Ruth never saw such a large mattress, such fine fabrics dressing one. How did he get it down here? She shivers in the bridal gown, which has sagged open wide as a trough at her neck. She can see right down the stretch of ribcage and navel to her bloomers. The belt is still secreted there, low on her hips, rat sack and sheathed knife: totems from her old life.

"Come, Bride," says Father Ernst. He tugs a short chain, and a square of wall opens. A hidden alcove. Inside, a cut-glass bottle. He unscrews the lid, pours a golden measure into one cup, pours more into a second. He hands Ruth the smaller portion. "A toast."

Ruth sniffs, wrinkles her nose. It's like the syrup they used to take to quiet their coughs at night.

"Sip," he says.

When she swallows, liquid fire burns its way from throat to belly. She smacks her lips, frowns.

Father Ernst chuckles. "Oak cask bourbon, a small and very good batch. Acquired taste, I suppose. This is near the last of it." He holds it in his mouth, savouring, just as he does his meals.

The second sip tastes better, and the sting of heat spreads across Ruth's chest.

"Did Mother Hannah tell you what to expect tonight?"

She shakes her head. "Only to do as you say."

"There's a little more to it than that." He sits on the bed, facing her. He strokes his beard.

He doesn't say anything else, not right away, so she drains her glass. Her fingers shake when she sets the cup down. Liquor zips through her. She feels taller. Braver. Dizzy.

Father Ernst pats the mattress beside him. Her fists clench at her sides. His lazy lids droop, but his eyes track her every movement.

"Are you teasing me, Wife?" He takes another amber sip.

Inside her, something begins to shout. "I don't feel good," she says.

"You pretend innocence, yet you seduce." His cheeks are pink from the liquor or from some great anticipation. Tongue tip to lip through the moustache. "Take off that gown, Temptress."

Does she hold a seditious spark to blaze the loins of men? Impossible. Yet there he sits, expectant. As though she knows what she's supposed to do. As though it's her choice, after all. Her legs are cement, thighs plastered together, crumbling. She cannot step out of the dress. She will not lift it.

"Ruth."

She licks her dry lips. Looks to her empty cup. Surprises them both by beginning to cry.

The spell is broken. Father Ernst sets down his glass, ruffles his hair. "Now, now," he says. "A little water?"

She nods. She's thirstier than before the drink and her head spins.

Father Ernst pulls his bookcase away from the wall and presses something she can't see. A hidden door swings open. "I keep a few things in here."

It's a storage closet, shelves stacked with provisions.

She steps closer. "Is that—is that food?" She wipes her face with the back of her hand. There are neatly labelled trays. Army-green canisters. Containers of water. He opens a new gallon jug. It's clear. Clean. He pours some into her cup, and she sucks it back, wipes her lips. Holds out the cup again.

"You can have more, after."

After what? But she knows. She must remove the dress. Get into the bed. He will touch her. He will do things to her body. Put part of himself inside her, into that tiny place she knows almost nothing about. Hannah said it will hurt and she might bleed but that it gets easier in time. She said, "Sometimes you might even like it."

Father Ernst tightens the lid and sets the water jug down. "I keep my women happy," he says with his wide pulpit smile.

"What about your children?" she blurts. Each little face lines up in her mind, desperate for clean water. While they shrivel to bone in their cold room, Father Ernst camps like a king, drinking, eating his secret supplies. Fury casts a winged cloak upon her: oh, how she rages now.

"You have food and water! Yet you deny us."

"It's not like that," he says.

Her eyes dart. "What else do you have? Are those guns?"

He shuts the door.

She gulps air. "Paul was right."

"He is born of his father's demon seed, evidenced by his black hair and wicked heart. We may each have our soulless hour, but we shall have our—"

"Deliverance." She spits the word like bad porridge.

"Cousin. You're a woman now. Woman's rage is more fierce than man's because she cannot understand." He taps his fingertips together. "These are Sacred provisions. God alone tells me when we may use them."

"Lies," she shouts. He reaches for her. Ruth's arms flail. She trips on the too-long skirt. He catches her waist and she pushes back against him. "I believed you! I defended you!" She is really crying now, snotty, with loud hiccups, and he crushes her against his chest.

"Shh," he says as he roughly pulls her onto his lap, onto the bed. His baritone deafens her, his stink smothers. He says, "Resistance is sin. It is the mind closing, the spirit dying. I cannot bear it. Resistance will destroy us. Are you infected? For shame, woman, for shame."

Shame. That word seeps through to her bones.

"Don't you love the Family? Don't you trust the Doctrine?"

"Yes. But—"

"But nothing." His profile—cliff-drop nose perched above sunken stone lips. "If you refuse to be mine, I must cast you out. Tonight."

Cast out? Alone, topside, where the sun burns a wicked inferno all hours of the day and lawless night while demons stalk the earth and evil prevails. She whispers, "I'm not a Philistine."

"Aren't you? Wearing trousers, carrying on like a man. Playing your games with me. I'll not be fooled by Lilith lies and crocodile tears. Defying God's will. Perhaps the Underworld will claim you instead of me."

His eyes look past, unfocused, as though he is seeing something else beyond her.

She pushes against him. "No."

"Whores and witches have no say among us." Beads of sweat stand on his forehead.

"I'm neither!"

"Yet you refuse me. Accuse me. Who do you think you are?" Hands move to her throat, closing around it. "Memaw weeps. How your Judas father rousted our only daughter away, it's still a mystery."

"You're my Father. I have no other," she says, and then there's no more air.

Nerves tick under Father Ernst's pouchy eye when he squeezes tighter. "And the tongue is a fire, a world of iniquity: that it defileth the body and setteth on fire the course of nature, and it is set on fire by Hell!" His hands squeezing her neck, he shakes her like a doll, and her braids sway. Eyes bulge. She strikes, tries to kick. Every ounce of her fights. Her vision begins to fade, and she slumps into his grip. His breath comes ragged, his arms shake—she draws her skirts up a little bit for him, and he relents.

"There's a good girl," he sighs, laying her back on the bed.

She's coughing, retching, desperate for air. Large hands drop on her, one on her chest, one pulling her thighs apart. Beard scratches her bare skin.

Help me, she prays. But there's no one.

He closes his eyes. Moustache parts to yellow teeth. His mating face, dear God. She's past this part already, out of her body. She's her own ghost, older even than him. Her hand snakes under the skirt, finds the belt. Unsheathes her knife. Hand on the grip.

Blade tip held to his torso, she hisses, "Stop."

His eyes widen. Palms raise, warming on an invisible fire. The white of his skin, his hair and beard, makes the whole room darker. "Put that down," he says.

"No."

His weight shifts and the blade tip sinks a little, tearing the fabric of his robe. His face slackens with disbelief. He slaps her arm and falls onto her with all of his weight. Ruth is pinned, her arm stretched wide, the knife flattened uselessly. "Jezebel!" Father Ernst heaves onto his back, pulling her halfway upright. Her skirts are caught under him; she can't get free. He lands a punch on her throbbing temple and she falls forward. The knife is still there on the bed, and she reaches for it, she holds it in both hands, and with a thrust, it is up to the handle in his hot stink. His eyes roll, hands curl to protect his guts. Ruth pulls out the dirty knife. For one moment, they both stare at the stain oozing through the fabric, the gore pooling.

"Repent!" cries Ruth.

Howls let loose from him. Hands beat at her. She forces the knife again, wet and deep. He keens, that tuneless high-pitched sorrow, thrashing on the bed. She is buffeted, bruised, but the knife lands true. She unzips her gown the rest of the way and, in her plain slip, struggles free.

Ruth runs to the door. The handle turns, but the door won't budge. Something's blocking it. She bangs and pounds against the door, screeches, and it creeps open a tiny bit. Through the crack she sees their large dining table propped close. Silas is waiting. He drags the heavy wooden table away, one inch at a time.

"Keys," he shouts. "Get the keys!"

Ruth twists and the room spins round and round. Keys. Father Ernst writhes on the bed, groaning. She tiptoes close and pats the sides of his robe. He swipes the air between them. Ruth shakes the stained fabric but there's no jingle, no weight from holding the key ring. *Think.* The sound of keys shifting when he leaned to kiss her during the ceremony. As they hopped and swayed during the dance. But not when he sat on his bed, not when he opened the hidden door, and not when they fought. Ruth scans Father's chamber. Framed photos, desk is bare, bed sheets a jumble, carpet rumpled on the floor. Keys—the ring is suspended from a lone nail on the wall beside the door. How did she miss it? It fits around her wrist like a charm bracelet.

"The children," she shouts to Silas. Now that she's free, he pushes the table back against Father Ernst's bedroom door, barricading him in.

"Susan took them to the Mission Pole."

Ruth runs the corridor faster than the old man ever could. Her body tingles with the hot pulse of power, harder than cement, darker than death. Heat bursts from the tight spot in her chest. She passes the cairn. The ladder is just ahead. She leans forward, gasping. She cannot hear for the pulse rushing through her ears. Tiny faces come into focus: the terrified children clutching Hannah's hands in the shadows.

Susan says, "Mind you take them up. I'll stay with Father."

Ruth shakes her head, but Susan thrusts Leah at her, and the little girl hugs onto her back. Ruth's bloody hands slip on ladder rungs. She sheathes the knife, wipes her hands on the cotton slip. She squeezes Leah's tiny hands clasped about her neck. Susan flicks her apron at them and, gasping for breath, Ruth begins to climb. Her strength wanes at the seventh rung.

"Lazy," shouts Susan, and that spurs her on.

Here comes Silas, stampeding the tunnel. Dust billows up the hatch, coats Ruth's teeth, sticks to her swollen, drying tongue. On the ninth rung, she begins to cough.

"Ruth!"

Slowly, she climbs.

There is darkness and there is the light—one lamp circle below when she peers down. In it, moths, the flutter of pale skirts. Bare and stockinged feet crowd around the ladder. Silas and Susan lift the twins, and they scramble up the rungs. Hannah carries Abel. Skirts flick above the lamp, shadows lurch high up the hatch. Elbows, fists, and feet work to climb careful steps. Little cries rise up.

Finally, Ruth reaches the handle, and while Leah breathes hot in her ear, Ruth slides the bolt, turns the key in the lock. Pushes the heavy door. There's a catch. The seal breaks, but the hinges stick. She pushes again, puts her injured self to it, all the want in the world, all the faith she ever had. It gives.

ACKNOWLEDGMENTS

I am grateful to the Canada Council for the Arts for generous financial support of this project. Thank you also to the Ontario Arts Council Writers' Reserve grant, recommended by ChiZine Publications. The Banff Centre for Arts and Creativity (in particular Wired Writing, under Fred Stenson's fine direction) and the Hambidge Center for Creative Arts and Sciences in Georgia are artists' refuges; a great deal of this book was dreamed up and written in their respective residency programs. I am deeply indebted to the generous and insightful Marina Endicott, who lent her careful eye and gave invaluable time and attention to early drafts of this work.

Esteemed writers who gave thoughtful consideration and encouragement to various drafts—including my dread bantling attempts—include Carolyn Beck, Anne Laurel Carter, Paige Cooper, Jani Krulc, Kanaga Kulendran, Frances Key Phillips, and Shannon Quinn. I am humbled by and grateful for their support over the years. Special thanks to Frances Key Phillips for graciously hosting the inaugural Little Stones reunion, and to Anne Laurel Carter for sharing her beautiful home in Nova Scotia. Thank you to Sarah Selecky, who published an excerpt in her Author's Spotlight series, and to Annetta Dunnion, who shared personal knowledge of quilting techniques and tradition. Marita Dachsel's *Glossolalia* compelled me to dig deeper into the lives of my fictional wives. I was lured into the survivalists' parallel universe by Neil Strauss's *Emergency*, and am forever changed.

Big Love to the incredible Arsenal Pulp Press team—Brian Lam, Oliver McPartlin, Cynara Geissler, and especially my editor Susan Safyan, whose kind and careful attentions enriched this book—it is such a pleasure to work with you.

To my parents, Annetta and Patrick Dunnion, for their steadfast support; my siblings and their remarkable families for timely distractions; and John MacDonald, for keeping it real.

PHOTO: LIZ MARSHALL

KRISTYN DUNNION's most recent novel *The Dirt Chronicles* (Arsenal Pulp Press) was a 2012 Lambda Literary Award Finalist. Previous novels include *Mosh Pit*, *Missing Matthew*, and *Big Big Sky* (Red Deer Press). Dunnion is the 2015 Machigonne Fiction prize winner and a Pushcart Prize nominee. She lives in Toronto